POSSESSIVE CAPTOR

A DARK MAFIA ROMANCE

THE VALENTI CRIME FAMILY
BOOK ONE

KELSIE CALLOWAY

CONTENTS

RANIERO

Every story needs a hero and a villain. In this story, I'm both.

The officer screaming at me has a piece of spinach stuck in his teeth. Or perhaps it's lettuce. I've been staring at the same green vegetable wedged between his canine and a crooked incisor for fifteen minutes and I still can't figure out what it is. His breath is oddly fruity—as if he had a strawberry vinaigrette on the salad that's clinging to his pearly whites.

"Do you hear me?" He leans in closer and I get a whiff of a nutty aroma to go with the spittle he flings at my cheek. "Are you listening to me, Valenti?"

I bring my finger up to my mouth and indicate toward the teeth I've been staring at for the last few minutes. "You've got something right there." I cluck my tongue. "Do you have any floss or anything? It's bothering me. I can get it for you if you'd like."

The officer pulls back as though he's been scalded with hot water. His cheeks turn a fire engine red and the vein in his forehead pops out. "Fuck you, Valenti."

"I just thought I should tell you. It's embarrassing to have food stuck in your teeth. I can't believe your little officer friends out there didn't tell you." As I shake my head, I cluck my tongue in disappointment. "You should find new friends, Officer Goodwin. Ones that will tell you when you look like an ass."

That must be where the invisible line between being a nice guy and being a jerk gets crossed. Officer Goodwin slams his hands down on the metal table between us and starts snarling insults at me.

In between a diatribe about *people like me* and *pieces of shit like me*, I snap my fingers in recognition. "The Pecanberry Salad!" I announce loudly, cutting him off. "That's what you had for lunch. That's a good one. When I'm on a health kick and want something a little sweeter, that's always what I order from—"

"Shut the fuck up, Valenti. Jesus Christ," he swears. "You're here to be questioned about a murder, not to become my personal dentist."

I hold my hand out in front of me and inspect my nails. They haven't been trimmed or buffed in a while, so they're looking a little long. I ought to cut these soon before I *actually* commit the crime I'm being accused of and accidentally get DNA trapped under them. "I told you once and I'll tell you again, I was at a school fundraiser when this alleged murder took place. You can call Bluemont Elementary school and ask them. Three of my cousin's kids go there and—"

Officer Goodwin cuts me off again. I know I did it to him once, but now he's just being rude. "I don't care how many of your sniveling little cousins go to Bluemont. You did it, Raniero. We know you did it. We have you on camera beating the victim in the head with a baseball bat."

I look up from examining my fingernails to meet the Officer's eyes. "Edward, you and I both know that wasn't me."

He gets flustered when I call him by his first name. "That's Officer—"

"—Goodwin," I finish for him with a roll of my eyes. "We both know that if I was going to dispose of someone, I wouldn't use a baseball bat. For starters, that's going to cause too much blood splatter and I'm not really a *clean the scene* kind of guy. I'd give him a few good licks to the face and then slam his head into the concrete until he stopped breathing."

Edward Goodwin looks like he's about to jump up and down in excitement; he probably thinks I'm admitting to a murder I *did* do. But the people I take care of don't get found by the police. "*If* I was going to murder someone, of course," I tack onto the end. "I'm but a humble businessman, Officer. As Bluemont Elementary might support considering I was issued a tax receipt upon my sizable donation to the school. I gave them my federal EIN and everything."

If they brought me in here because of a crime I'd *actually* committed, I'd have my lawyer by my side. But the victim in question is someone I've never had a connection to. The paperwork in the file folder on the table contains trumped-up evidence of our many meetings, but I've never seen the deceased in my life. They're framing me. The problem is I don't know why.

Before Officer Goodwin can lose his cool again, the door to the interrogation room opens and reveals the Chief of Police. I've had several encounters with Grant Jackson over the years and I have to admit, he's in the best shape of his life. When we first met fifteen years ago when he was starting out, he packed on a freshman fifteen like I'd never seen before. He must have a new woman in his life if he's shedding the pounds and saying no to donuts.

"I'll finish this up," Grant says with a nod in Edward's direction.

The police officer glares at me as if he has more to say. When I give him a stupid, carefree smile, it almost seems like he might jump across this metal table and strangle me. But Edward's Chief is watching the two of us and he settles for pointing an accusatory finger at me and saying, "You're going to slip up one day, Valenti, and we're going to get your ass once and for all."

I wave goodbye as he exits the room. Poor guy. He's been here for a decade and wasted all of his best years issuing traffic citations and catching drunk drivers. "Chief Jackson," I smile as he shuts the door behind his coworker. "It's good to see you again. I hope you're here to spring me from the joint. You and I both know I didn't do this."

Grant quietly walks over to the table and reaches under the bottom right-hand corner. I hear a small, almost indiscernible click as he flips a switch. "This is off the record," he says as he takes a seat in front of me.

"Oh, yeah?" I lean forward in excitement. "Are you going to ask me to infiltrate a gang? Commit a few crimes to keep an eye on if your guys are doing their job? Because as long as you clear my record, I'm happy to help you out."

He steeples his fingers together in front of his face as he stares at me. "All you had to do was take the fall for this. We'd have sent you up the river, you would have done the time, and we'd have left the Valenti crime family alone."

A mock frown appears on my face. "Up the river? There isn't even a river nearby, Chief. I think you're mixing metaphors."

A smile tugs on the corners of his lips as he shakes his head in frustration. "You can never keep your mouth shut, can you?"

I cluck my tongue and lean away from him, my back coming in contact with the uncomfortable metal chair I've been sitting in for over an hour now. "'Fraid not. But I reckon if I did, you guys would sure pin a hell of a lot more on me than I'm capable of."

Grant audibly snorts as he rolls his eyes. I must admit that for a man almost turning fifty, he has great command over his body language and facial expressions. He doesn't give away anything that he doesn't want me to know about. "I know what you're capable of, Raniero, believe me. Just because you didn't kill this guy doesn't mean someone in your little family isn't responsible."

If one of my guys beat someone to death in a well-lit, photographed alley, he's stupid and he deserves to spend the rest of his life behind bars. "Be careful with your accusations, Chief. The Valenti's are big supporters of this town. We've always donated to the police fund even when your guys pull stupid shit like accusing me of a murder I clearly have an alibi for." My joking tone is suddenly more serious. This is the first time since I was picked up off the street by a fucking traffic cop that I'm done playing games. "The next time one of your officers hauls me in for questioning of a crime I had nothing to do with, I'll bring my lawyer in to draw up papers to sue this department. Are we clear?"

I watch as his thick, disgusting tongue comes

out to wet his bottom lip. I want to reach across the table and grab it right out of his mouth. He'd be better off if he couldn't speak.

"You should have just taken the fall, Raniero. Because now I'm going to investigate every Italian in the city and if I have to throw people in jail over unpaid parking tickets or jaywalking, I'll do it." Grant stands up and leans his weight onto the table. "I will bring down the Valenti family one by one if I have to. Eventually, someone is going to crack under the strain of questioning. That's when I'll bring you down. If it's the last thing I do, I'll see your ass behind bars."

If my lawyer were here, he'd advise to me keep my mouth shut and wait for them to release me. But my lawyer is in Boca Raton and the only thing stopping me from snapping the neck of this insolent Police Chief is the fact that I'm on his turf.

I match his body language and get to my feet, leaning forward until our faces are only a few inches apart. "You do what you have to do, Grant, but remember that your actions have consequences. If you want to threaten my family, you better protect yours. Because I'm coming for *everyone* you're related to."

"You hurt my family and I'll kill you in broad

daylight with a crowd watching. No one will find me guilty when I tell them what you did." Grant turned off the recorder in the room when he arrived because he knew what was going to happen. He knew that he was going to waltz in here, throw out a few threats, and hope I said or did something that could get me arrested.

But I've never been easy to capture or kill and I'm not starting today. "Who said anything about hurting them?"

A plan is already formulating. I'll need to do a background check to find out where his wife and kids are. If I have to traipse halfway across the country to find them in their college dorms, I'll do it. No one threatens the Valenti family on my watch.

2

CALLIOPE

In second grade when the teacher asked what we wanted to be when we grew up, I didn't say realtor. No one did. But now that we're adults, our faces are everywhere.

Mine decorates half a dozen lawns in Manhattan, all with a price point of $250,000 or less. The commission from selling any of those homes would keep me afloat for a couple of months, but in the meantime, I'm couch surfing and living off the goodwill of my friends.

But today everything is going to change; I can feel it. The scent of budding flowers is in the air and my newest listing is buzzing. A Sunday open house often brings in the neighbors and the nosy, but there are a few interested parties this afternoon.

And frankly, who wouldn't be interested? Sharon Ray is selling her bi-level split four-bedroom, three-bathroom home for less than market value. The curb appeal is promising as the house resides in a coveted neighborhood. All the appliances were replaced within the last year and the kitchen had a full renovation three years ago. Everything about this place reeks of money and privilege—and worth at least $50,000 more.

But if the people peeking in her drawers and looking through her closets knew that she was selling this place because her husband fucked the neighbor on the shiny new kitchen island, they might show a little less enthusiasm. In lieu of the whole truth, I tell the potential buyers strolling through the house that the seller is upgrading. That isn't a lie. With a cheating husband and a neighbor that can't keep her hands off other peoples' property, getting a divorce and buying a new house *is* an upgrade.

When 2:00 pm rolls around, it comes with a burst of new potential buyers. All are couples, but they range across very different walks of life. One man asks if I can give him my client's number. When I turn him down, he huffs, grabs his girlfriend, and storms out. If he's looking to undercut my sale by negotiating directly with the seller, he's got the wrong girl.

The truth is I like being a realtor. It isn't my dream job, but it has its perks. I make my own schedule and can come in as early or as late as I want. I do have to work some weekends, but it's never all day. I get to spend time outside and I'm always meeting new people. The commissions aren't bad either—*when* you sell a house, of course.

"Ma'am," a woman snaps her fingers to get my attention and I consider ignoring her. I am not a dog to be summoned and sent away at will. "Ma'am, how many other people have put an offer in on this house?"

I can't tell her that. Nor can I tell her what those offers are even if there were any. The house *just* went on the market thirty-six hours ago; does she expect people to have made offers already? This isn't the height of the pandemic when homes were sold within four hours. "I'm afraid I can't share that information." I paste a smile on my face and stare at the hideous broach on her chest.

"But you *do* have offers," she says snidely. "That'll be all." Her tone is dismissive. It makes me want to cross the living room and slap the smug look off her face.

While this job has its perks, it has its downsides, too. Like dealing with jerks that think it's your job to kiss their ass and get them whatever they want. I might work on commission, but my soul is worth more than a few thousand dollars. I won't be mistreated to earn a couple of bucks. I'm not that desperate. Anymore, anyway.

As the minutes pass, the guests filter out little by little until it's 2:45 and the last couple has left. I could shut the open house down early and take those extra fifteen minutes for myself; it's not as though anyone would know. But just as I'm contemplating locking all the doors and leaving, a car pulls up in front of the property. A black Tesla from the look of it.

I mess with the papers on the counter that highlight the details of the house while I wait for the prospective buyer to come in. I'm surprised to see a single man get out of the car, but maybe his wife is meeting him in a few minutes or perhaps she's working. Nonetheless, I pull a smile onto my face when he walks through the door.

"Am I too late?" He asks as he crosses the threshold. He looks around the living room until he spots me in the kitchen. "I can set up an appointment if that would be easier."

I come from behind the island and give him a dismissive wave. He seems nice enough with an easygoing smile and unassuming body language. "No, come in," I usher him forward. "A lot of people came before or after church, so you're probably lucky you came so late. There are significantly fewer people here than an hour ago."

The man breathes a sigh of relief and gently closes the door behind him. "Great. Thanks! My wife told me to drop by earlier, but I lost track of time. She wouldn't have forgiven me if I didn't check this place out in person."

Though his salt and pepper locks make me think he's in his forties, for a moment after he walked through the door, I thought he was attractive. That comes to a screaming halt when he mentions his wife, though I must admit that I don't see a ring on his finger. "You're welcome to walk around and check the place out. If you have any questions, let me know. It's a generous four-bedroom, three-bathroom home with plenty of space for a family. Do you have any kids?"

He looks around the open-concept living room and kitchen that flow seamlessly together. I notice the sharp line of his jaw beneath the freshly trimmed beard. "No, no kids yet. It's in the cards though," he mumbles as he walks over to the kitchen island and runs his fingers across the marble countertop. "Could you give me a tour?" When he looks up to meet my eyes, I catch a hint of embarrassment in his gaze. "I don't want to miss anything important. When my wife asks me what I saw, I want to be able to parrot your answers back to her."

I have nothing else to do. The alternative is to wait around in the kitchen for him to finish checking out the downstairs. "I'm happy to be of assistance. I'm Calliope, by the way."

He pushes a hand in my direction while wearing a charming smile that nearly takes my breath away. "Raniero," he introduces himself. "Calliope is such a pretty name."

I give his hand a shake before waving him forward to follow me to the master bedroom in the hallway of the kitchen. "My mother had a thing for Greek names. I have twin older brothers named Ares and Apollo." She wanted to name me Athena, originally, but my father vetoed it.

"Wow, this is huge," Raniero changes the subject as we enter the master bedroom.

"It's 350 square feet of living space complete with two walk-in closets and an on-suite bathroom.

In fact," I start walking toward the bathroom, "the owners installed a beautiful soaking tub a few years ago with built-in jets. Your wife will love coming home after a long day and relaxing in her own personal spa."

I feel Raniero's presence in the bathroom before I turn around and see him. I direct his gaze toward the massive bathtub kept immaculately clean by the current owners. "And, as you can see, the shower is a good size as well." The master bathroom would sell anyone on this home. It comes with dual vanities, plenty of under-counter storage space, and a closed-off water closet that houses the toilet. "I believe the owners renovated the bathroom bit by bit over the last decade, but as you can see, they took very good care of the space."

Raniero touches everything, even the monogrammed towels hanging by the shower. His eyes appraise the value of each addition made by the owners and he nods in appreciation of their taste. "This is heaven. Who would ever want to leave?"

Once again I keep Sharon Ray's dirty laundry to myself. "They're looking to upgrade," I tell him swiftly.

He leads me back into the bedroom and makes a beeline for the closet. I've seen inside of it half a dozen times. The space is bigger than the bathroom in my last apartment and it's lined with pristine white shelves and blonde wood railings. There is more invested in the clothes in Sharon's closet than anyone has ever invested in me.

"What's this?" Raniero asks from inside the closet.

I suspect he means the square cut-out in the back corner. If you push the cut-out up, you'll be given access to the attic. I'm just about to tell him that when I enter the closet and see him pointing a gun at me.

"Don't scream, Calliope," he says immediately. Gone is the genial tone he spoke in when he first arrived. In its place is a menacing inflection that brokers no room for arguing.

"I don't have any money," I tell him as I hold my hands up by the sides of my head. My heart feels like it's about to pound out of my chest.

Raniero takes a step forward and I do the opposite. "Don't move," he instructs. Then he steps toward me again and reaches out to drag his hand across my cheek. "You're a beautiful girl, Calliope. I'm surprised you don't bring protection to open houses."

There is a stun gun in my car and pepper spray

on my keychain. Unfortunately, my keys are on the kitchen counter and my car is in the driveway; neither are close enough for me to use them. "The owners are going to be home soon." I can't take my eyes off the gun at his hip pointed at my stomach.

"Really? I thought Sharon was in Bermuda on vacation while you sold her house." How does he know her name? I mean, I'm sure it's public record, but no one looks up the owner of the house they're potentially interested in. "And if I remember correctly, Christopher doesn't even live here anymore. He was kicked out, wasn't he?"

I tear my eyes away from the gun long enough to meet Raniero's gaze. "How do you know all this?"

He shrugs his shoulders, leaving a wrinkle in the black shirt he's wearing. "When you're friends with the homeowners, you know a lot of things the general public doesn't."

Oh, god. He's one of their neighbors, maybe even the husband of the woman that got caught cheating by Sharon. "Listen, I'm just doing my job," I explain, "I don't know anything about the owners' personal lives or—"

"Save it," Raniero cuts me off as he lets his hand fall from my face. "I don't care about Sharon or Christopher anymore than I care about the thirty-two fucking people who toured the house earlier today. The only thing I care about is you."

My palms are sweaty and I swear the dampness between my breasts comes from fear. "Wh-what do you want?" I ask, determined to give him whatever it is he requests.

Raniero grabs my wrist and turns me around. With my back facing him, I nearly piss myself when I feel the tip of the gun press into my spine. "I want you to walk out to my car and get inside without screaming or making a fuss. If I think you're trying to get someone's attention or if I catch you yelling for help, I'll bury a bullet into your back and make sure that you never walk again."

I stand there frozen in fear until he shoves the gun forward, forcing me to take a step.

"Do you understand me, Calliope Jackson?" He knows who I am. My name is on the sign outside, but I don't think it's a coincidence.

"What do you want from me?" I ask again as I take one tentative step after another.

He's on me like a second skin. The hand that grabbed my wrist and twisted me around now rests on my hip. "Revenge."

3

RANIERO

It's taken me three months to get everything in place, starting with finding out the most vulnerable member of Grant Jackson's family.

It turns out he had a wife a couple of decades ago, but she left him and their family to get away from his abuse. I read the reports and it turns out Grant was one of the 40% of officers that engage in domestic violence. When his wife fled the home, he tried to force her to court to demand her return or some child support, but she fell off the map. One day she was running for her life, the next day she disappeared into thin air as though she never existed.

Grant has a pair of twin boys, 29, that left

Manhattan, Kansas for The Big Apple. They went to the real Manhattan and make their living in finance. Ares is married with three kids and Apollo has one on the way. I could have gone after the two of them, but I make it a priority not to hurt children.

I settled for his daughter, a 25-year-old that he has no contact with. According to the sealed police records, she had one hell of a crime spree in her youth. She vandalized buildings, stayed out past curfew, ran with a few gangs, stuck up a gas station, and more. I guess because her daddy was the Chief of Police, he got a lot of those charges dismissed or downgraded so that her name wouldn't be splashed across the papers.

Calliope's trail ran cold after her high school graduation, but Manhattan is a small town. If you ask around enough, you can find out anything about anyone. Including information about the girl that ran away from home at seventeen and spent the last eight years living in poverty or just above it.

She might not have any communication with her father, but I bet that's because he pulled the same shit with her that he did with his ex-wife. Her mom left when she was five years old and that certainly fucks a person up. But being beaten and verbally abused certainly leaves its marks. There's no way Calliope Jackson, spelling bee champion of her sixth-grade class, went to junior high and suddenly started rolling with gangbangers for fun. Something changed during the summer because it wasn't until fall that her rap sheet started collecting incidents.

For the past year, she's been working on getting her real estate license. Calliope had a friend in the business that was willing to front her the money for classes and exams if she paid her back from her future commissions. I found the friend a few weeks ago and paid off Calliope's debt. She'd barely entered the business, but I wanted her to start out with a clean slate. Not to mention the fewer people who came looking for her, the better.

Getting her in the right place at the right time became crucial. I had to set her up in a quiet little neighborhood where no one would be peeking through their curtains and find me carrying her off. That's when Christopher Ray's name came across my desk.

Christopher Ray was a high-profile lawyer in Manhattan that dealt with estate planning and administration. Two years ago he'd fucked one of my friends out of their inheritance due to a loophole in the law. While I made sure my friend received financial compensation for her loss, I kept Christopher's name in a book. One day I'd bring him down.

You know what they say about two birds and one stone. My 'in' was the Ray family. All it took was a few chats with the neighbor to convince her to hit on Chris. She said they already flirted over yard work anyway. I watched from down the street as he impaled her on the kitchen island right in front of the living room window. Perhaps if it hadn't been dark outside and he hadn't turned on all the lights, I wouldn't have been able to see him fuck her like a bitch in heat.

The pièce de résistance was Sharon coming home early and walking in on them. When she found the neighbor with her tits pressed against their marble countertops, she lost it. It was almost funny to see plates fly and shatter when they hit a wall. I bet the inside of that place was covered in glass and ceramic for weeks.

But Sharon was easily led to Foundation Realty. Her listing fell in Calliope's hands and therefore the open house fell in mine. Three months of planning went into being in the right place at the right time.

. . .

"This is your room." I tuck the gun back into its holster at my waist. "The door locks from the outside. Eventually, you'll be allowed to roam the house on your own, but not right now. You're a flight risk."

Calliope was quiet the entire drive here. I'm certain she was trying to figure out a way out of the car. I was waiting for her to try and open the door and tuck and roll at a stoplight, but she never did. "What am I doing here?"

God, she asks the same question over and over again like a broken record. It's like she can't function without an answer. "I told you." I walk around the room and start flipping on the lights, showing her where her closet and bathroom are.

"Revenge," she responds in a dull sort of way. "But I don't know what that means."

Just tell her, the little voice in my head insists. He must be the angel that sits on your shoulder and tells you right from wrong. "You are Grant Jackson's daughter, correct?"

Calliope walks over to the window and takes a seat on the padded alcove. I watch as she takes the hem of her dress and plays with it between her fingers. "Are you a pissed off criminal or something? Because I don't talk to my dad. If you think you're going to use me for revenge, you're wrong. My father would rather watch me rot than save my life."

"I think you're mistaken. He'll come around when he knows that it was me who kidnapped you." Even if the only reason he tries to save Calliope is to send me to prison, he'll show up for his daughter.

My captive leans forward to look at the gardens beneath her window. "This is a nice home," she comments quietly.

Considering she's been sleeping on a friend's couch for the last three weeks, this is probably the nicest place she's stayed at since she lived with her father. "Enjoy the view, you're going to be looking at it for a while."

She sighs before turning her head to look at me. I get a glimpse of her emerald eyes when she meets my gaze. The framing of her dark, brunette locks around her face makes her skin look porcelain in this light. "How long am I going to be here? I'd like to adjust my expectations to match yours."

Calliope is very well-spoken and I must admit that I expected more of a fight from her. But she's probably just biding her time before she plots her escape attempt. She can attempt to leave all she wants; I will find her and I will bring her back here every time. "You're going to be here for the rest of your life."

Her brow furrows in confusion. "I thought you were waiting for my father to come around."

A smile touches my lips and it's a struggle to keep from revealing my entire plan to her right here, right now. "Yes, to come around to being my father-in-law and the grandpa to our children."

She grows pale and those emerald eyes practically double in size. It gives her a childlike appearance when her nose starts to turn red. Calliope opens her mouth to say something but struggles to find the right words. Like a fish gasping for water, her jaw moves up and down on a hinge.

"You should make yourself comfortable. You should have plenty of supplies in the bathroom, as well as clothes handpicked for you by my personal designer. I believe she got the right size, but if not, let me know and we can replace anything." A few pilfered clothes from her friend's poorly locked home were all that I needed to get her measurements. "There's a mini fridge in the closet along with a shelf full of snacks. You will have food and drink available to you at all times, but you'll dine with me for all meals."

It took me three months to make this happen.

Three months to have this room outfitted with the appropriate clothes, food, and supplies that Calliope would need. Three months to ensure that every weapon she could possibly create was removed. Three months to get everything in place.

I told Grant to protect his family and he didn't listen to me. Now his daughter is my captive and soon to be my wife.

Maybe he'll listen now.

4

———

CALLIOPE

*I*t could *always* be worse.

Three years ago I had to bear down under an overpass and wait for the tornado sirens to stop going off. The wind was whipping around like crazy throwing dirt and rocks at my face and I was there with half a dozen other men and women. The weather people said the wind gusts got up to eighty miles per hour. But luckily, the threat of a tornado passed. They said one never touched down, but curled up in a little ball under that overpass, I beg to differ.

As I made my way back to my tent in the homeless camp just outside Manhattan, I saw rogue garbage cans, siding ripped off houses, and every manner of backyard furniture strewn across the streets. Not to mention the tree branches that littered almost every inch of the neighborhoods I walked through. It was a mess.

The homeless camp barely survived. A majority of our tents and items had gone flying across the field that spanned to the east of our site, but nothing major had disappeared. I gathered what items I could find and wound up stealing someone else's tent when I couldn't find mine, but no one ever approached me about it.

That wasn't the only time I was homeless, it was just the worst. I was kicked off a friend's couch after he returned home drunk from the bars one night and tried to climb under my blankets. When I told him that it wasn't like that between us, he told me to get out. At three in the morning, I gathered the few items I had and hit the streets. Thankfully, it was summer.

I spent three months living in that homeless

camp before I found a job that paid enough for me to get an apartment. It was only waitressing at Texas Roadhouse, but they were so busy that I collected enough tips to get myself a place in the most rundown part of the town. It was nicer than sleeping on the ground though.

Life hasn't been easy. I've gone through periods of wealth and periods of poverty, neither of which I'd choose to go through again.

At my most comfortable, I was twelve years old living at home with my father. My mother had disappeared a few years before, but we moved on. We *prevailed*, as dad would say. But that year I started blossoming. My body filled out and my face looked more mature than pudgy. One day my father came home from work, took one look at me, and brought the back of his hand across my jaw. It was all downhill from there.

At my lowest point, I was sleeping with a brick in the park praying that no one would find me. If the police came across me, they'd take me in, then I'd have to deal with my father taunting me. The brick was to protect myself against thieves and rapists, both of which existed in droves depending on the time of day. Thankfully, it was all uphill from there, I just didn't know it at the time.

A year ago a friend of mine, Cynthia, from high school found me working the front desk at a local hotel. She was there for a work conference when she stopped to chat with me for a bit. She talked about how she left high school not entirely knowing what she wanted to do with her life. Her parents were wealthy and they floated her along while she figured it out, but eventually, she settled into real estate. Now she had a husband and she was making $60,000 a year selling other people's homes. Cynthia claimed that it wasn't the wealth that she'd come from, but it was good enough for her.

I couldn't imagine what making $60,000 a year would be like. I could afford an apartment that didn't come with the threat of break-in any time I was gone. I could buy food every week instead of trying to ration the spinach I'd gotten from Aldi twelve days ago that was looking a little limp. I could probably even afford to keep my heat above 60 in the wintertime. If I could make $60,000 a year, I would be living large.

I called Cynthia the next day during my break. I didn't tell her about everything that had happened to me since high school, but I gave her enough details so that she could paint her own picture. I wasn't rich and I didn't need to be, I just wanted to make enough money to survive.

Cynthia mulled it over for a few days before returning to the hotel. She offered to pay for the classes I'd need to get my real estate license. She claimed that it was because we were such good friends back in high school and she couldn't bear to see me failing at life. I was just poor enough to take her up on the offer.

Life didn't magically change when I became a real estate agent. I didn't suddenly have all the money Cynthia bragged about. Instead, I had to wait six weeks before I sold my first home and then another two months on top of that before the commission came in. I was still working part-time at the hotel to pay my bills because no one said that being a realtor could make you rich or it could break you.

But when my first commission came in, 3% on a $225,000 home, I had enough money to take care of myself for the next three months. I couldn't buy name-brand food at Kroger, but I could fill my cart and not feel bad that I splurged on an extra box of granola bars.

I think with a couple more years, I could have

gotten to that coveted $60,000 number that Cynthia talked about. But now I'd never know.

Raniero drove me out past the lake. I watched Manhattan disappear in the rearview as he took me to his home. I could vaguely remember a news article saying *never let the kidnapper take you to a second location*, but I'd already fucked that up. He was racing down backroads and whistling along to the song on the radio. I thought when he got me to wherever he was taking me, he was going to rape me, kill me, and leave my body to be eaten by the coyotes.

Instead, he brought me to a sprawling home that I would have given my right arm to sell and get the commission on. It had to be at least 5,000 square feet if not more. The house had a view of the lake from one side and an expansive backyard that felt like it continued for miles. It was the nicest place I'd ever been in.

When he brought me to what would be my room, I almost felt like Cinderella. I'd been swept off my feet by a morally grey Prince Charming and he was turning my life upside down. I didn't want to think about it too much because that's when the realization kicked in that he had still kidnapped me and I had no idea what his plans for me were.

Until he spilled the beans, of course. Babies, marriage, and pissing off my father. It was one hell of a shock to the system.

But, as I'd told myself a thousand times since leaving my father's house at seventeen, it could *always* be worse.

Marrying Raniero could be exactly what I need to finally turn my life around. He's handsome, of course, even if he is a bit older than me. Despite the gun he shoved into my back at the open house, he was very gentle with me.

I never wanted to have kids. I couldn't imagine bringing anyone into this world when I was doing such a shit job of surviving already. But the money this man has *has* to count for something. He can financially take care of a child. He can even take care of me.

It could be worse. He could be a poor man holding me hostage in a shack trying to knock me up while living off of canned beans. Instead, he has me locked in a bedroom with temperature control, nice sheets, and a closet full of clothes handpicked for me.

This is every girl's dream, but mine, especially. I suffered under my father's abuse for five years. Surely I can handle whatever Raniero can throw my way in exchange for a warm bed and plenty of food in my stomach.

Surely...

5

RANIERO

Sampson brings Calliope to the dining room at 7:00 pm sharp, as requested. He holds an all-encompassing role as my bodyguard. He does my bidding in a number of situations, but his only part in my kidnapping is leading my victim around the house and making sure that she doesn't escape.

An hour ago one of the maids informed Calliope that dinner would be taking place soon and she needed to get ready. With a closet full of clothes at her disposal, she settled on a full-length skirt and a loose-fitting blouse. Neither item accentuates the curves she has beneath them, something I had a decent view of when she was dressed in her Sunday best for her open house, but that's okay. If she wants to wear something comfortable, I won't stop her.

Calliope steps over the threshold and I raise my hand to stop her in her tracks. "Get on your hands and knees."

A frown creases her forehead as she stands twenty feet from me on the other side of the kitchen. "Wh-what?"

It occurred to me while I was preparing my household for Calliope's arrival that she might try to earn our confidence in order to launch an escape attempt. I warned my staff that if they let her go, there would be hell to pay. But I thought long and hard about what I would need to do in order to break her of her natural inclinations to run.

"I said get on your hands and knees. I want you to crawl over to me." I settled for treating her like a dog. I might be marrying her and putting my Valenti baby inside of her, but she doesn't need to think that she has any control over me. I am the one in charge here.

Calliope struggles with the command for a few seconds before finally sinking to her knees on the other side of the kitchen. I see a pained look cross her face as she leans forward on her hands. Her cheeks flush with embarrassment when she takes a few slow crawls toward me. I never see her eyes because they're trained on the floor in disgrace.

She must not realize how beautiful she looks right now. Her body language is completely submissive as she makes her way over to me. The only way this could be sexier was if she was wearing nothing at all and was forced to crawl away from me. I would love to see her cunt twitch as she moved from limb to limb back to her bedroom.

The knees on her skirt must be painted in dirt by the time she arrives at my side. She looks up a little hesitantly as if to ask *what next?* Her natural inclination to submission makes my cock hard. "You can sit up now," I insist. "But you'll have to beg for scraps."

She's so red she looks like she might implode. It is a gorgeous color on her cheeks and I wonder what it would look like draped across other parts of her body. Calliope tightens her jaw and reconciles herself with the position she's found herself in. "Can I please have some food?" She asks after a moment.

I reach out to pat her on the head, dragging my hand down the side of her face as she kneels beside me. "We must start with our vegetables. It's an important part of a growing girl's body." I grab my fork from the side of my plate and use it to spear a couple strings of green beans, then I bring it down to her lips. "Blow on it," I tell her with a grin, "it's hot."

Her lips form a perfect, soft 'O' as she leans forward to blow on my forkful of green beans. She doesn't complain, she simply breathes cool air on the vegetables before opening her mouth and closing it around the tines.

I nearly have to adjust myself where I sit. All I'm imagining is her making that same motion around the tip of my cock. Her perfectly pink lips wrap around the head of my member as she tries to swallow me the way she swallows those green beans. I'm leaking pre-cum just thinking about it.

As she chews peacefully, I bring both hands to my plate to cut up the steak. After a few pieces, I bring one to my mouth to satiate my own needs. The flavor explodes on my tongue. "Delicious," I tell Calliope with a wink. "You're going to love it."

And indeed, her anger melts into resplendence when her mouth closes around the bite of steak that I offer her. Knowing her past, I know without question that this is already the nicest meal she's ever had, even if she's on her knees having it.

It's foreplay to watch her open and close her

mouth around every forkful of food that I offer her. The tightness of her jaw disappears after the first couple of bites and by the time we've shared my plate of food, she looks perfectly content. I hate to ruin it, but I have no other choice.

With only a few bites of mashed potatoes left and the steak drippings coating my plate, I set my fork down on the table. Slowly, I push my chair back and tilt it diagonally to face her. A hint of confusion rests in her gaze, but it's quickly replaced with fear when I reach forward and grab her face.

The bones of her jaw dig into my hand as I tighten my fingers around her cheeks. The tranquil dinner we just had is replaced with aggression and anxiety. "You've been a good little girl today, my pet." With my other hand, I reach up to stroke her hair. The brunette locks catch my digits between the strands, but I grab her hair and pull her toward me. "But if you want a spot at *my* table, you're going to have to earn it."

Calliope's eyes have widened as far as they'll go. She looks up at me in horror before I feel her jaw start to move. I loosen my grip enough for her to speak. "H-how?" Comes her timid response. "How do I earn it?"

If I would have found a woman as inclined to

obedience as Calliope, I would have married her instantly. Instead, I had to wait. It's been forty-one long years of dating, fucking, and leaving women who couldn't live up to my standards. All along, I just had to look a little closer at the circle I ran in. If I had known seven years ago when Calliope turned eighteen that she was exactly the woman I was looking for, I'd have lived a happier life.

"Are you still hungry?" She has to be; I am. We shared a plate meant for one.

After a moment, Calliope nods her head yes before following it up with a verbal agreement.

I release her face but keep my hand twisted in her hair. "Then take your fill of this." With my now free hand, I unbutton the top button of my pants.

Calliope's eyes watch my every movement and I swear I can hear her heart racing as she realizes what I'm asking of her. It takes her a moment, but when she meets my eyes again, it's with a trace of timidity in her gaze. "I-I-I," she starts to stutter before taking a deep breath. "I've never done that before," Calliope finally admits.

Fucking hell. It's been a long time since I popped a woman's throat cherry. In just a few seconds, she'll be choking on my thick, hard cock. My future wife... a blowjob virgin. But not for much longer.

I release my grip on her hair and sit back in my chair. I unzip my pants and pull my dick out for her. Her green eyes drift downward as I handle myself. "You're going to learn how to do it today," I tell her. "Now put daddy in your mouth and suck me like a lollipop."

Whatever she's thinking, she puts it aside as she leans forward and wraps her lips around my shaft like she did my fork. I'm treated to a porno as she fulfills my fantasies.

The back of her head bobs up and down on my cock until I'm ready to burst. Her teeth never touch me, but she swipes her tongue across my head at just the right time. For a woman that's never mouth fucked a man before, she sure knows exactly what to do to make me pop off.

I fill her throat with cum until she's pulling away from me and I see it dripping down her chin. God, she's a gorgeous creature. What I wouldn't do to see her pussy cream pied and dripping just like this.

Calliope brings the back of her hand up to her face and uses it to wipe off the remnants of my pleasure. I get up from my chair and lean down to place a kiss on the top of her head. "Sampson will bring you a plate of food. Feel free to sit at the table and enjoy it. Good night, my love."

I need a cold shower before I rip Calliope off the floor, throw her on the dining table, and fuck her senseless.

6

CALLIOPE

ow put daddy in your mouth and suck me like a lollipop.

I don't know if I'll ever go through another day without hearing those words ring through my thoughts.

I tentatively lean forward and replace the hand on his cock with my own. The skin is soft, like velvet, encasing his rock-hard enthusiasm. Something inside of me snaps as I arch toward his member.

I lick my lips quickly before stretching them over his tip. My jaw feels strained at being open this wide, but I push the frisson of pain to the back of my thoughts.

As I inch down further on his dick, I have to hide my teeth behind my lips to keep from brushing them along the sensitive skin of his shaft. I could bite down right now, leaving him screaming in pain as I hightail it away from his mansion. But I bet he'd find me and do worse than lock me in a nice room and force me to crawl on my knees to get my supper.

I don't know what I'm doing, but Raniero makes sounds as if he enjoys it. He gathers my hair in a fist, pulling it back from my face so he can get a better view of his cock disappearing inside my mouth. I hear a strained curse word slip from his lips.

My tongue feels useless in my mouth as I take him as far back as I can manage. The tip of his cock triggers my gag reflex and I choke on him. My throat tightens around him as the few bites of dinner I had threaten to reappear. But just as quickly as I'm suffocating around him, he uses his grip on my hair to yank my head back.

I linger on the top half of his dick for a few moments as I try to regain my senses. I run my tongue along the underside of his shaft and hear him start praising Mary and Joseph. I think that's a good sign.

When I feel comfortable taking him in my mouth again, I bob up and down on his member. My movements are shallow at first, not wanting to choke again, but Raniero forces my head down further until I feel him tickling the back of my throat again.

"Fuck," he swears loudly, the word ringing off the walls of the dining room. A second later, he explodes in my mouth. The taste of his salty sperm coats my mouth and I don't know what to do. I want to sit back and let him finish elsewhere, but his grip on my hair makes that impossible. Instead, I swallow as fast as I can. He doesn't taste gourmet like the steak he was just feeding me, but he isn't bad.

Raniero finally releases my hair and it falls around my shoulders like a curtain. I pull away from him and cum dribbles out of my mouth. What I couldn't swallow fast enough now drips down my chin and I bring my hand up to surreptitiously wipe it away.

When he gets up, he leans down to press his lips to the top of my head. It is an intimate gesture that sends a shiver down my spine. "Sampson will bring you a plate of food," Raniero says after a moment, his voice taking on a very serious tone. "Feel free to sit at the table and enjoy it. Good night, my love." Then he leaves the room, the soles of his shoes echoing through the hallway before he makes it to the staircase.

A second later, Sampson appears with a covered silver tray. "Miss Jackson," he nods his head at me, "I was instructed to give this to you."

I get to my feet and my legs feel a little wobbly. My knees hurt, but that's to be expected after kneeling on marble for the last half hour. I take the seat that Raniero was just in as Sampson removes the first plate and leaves mine in its wake. "Thank you," I mumble quietly.

Sampson nods his head once before backing out of the room. There's no one around, but it still feels like someone's eyes are on me. I grab the steak knife left on the table and the fork Raniero and I both shared. Between the two, I cut into the divine, medium-rare treasure before me. Despite having a belly full of cum and half a plate of steak and potatoes, my stomach rumbles when I bring the tines to my lips. This was definitely worth losing my blowjob virginity over.

As I'm escorted upstairs a few minutes later when I'm too stuffed to keep eating, I take stock of the mansion bathed in gold from the setting sun. Priceless paintings hang on the wall. Every inch of the downstairs floor is covered in cold, beautiful marble. Ornate hardware is everywhere: door handles, drawer handles, cabinet pulls, and more. Everything is coated in a layer of wealth and privilege that, even when I was living with my father, I never experienced.

"What does Raniero do?" I ask Sampson. He holds me by the bicep and for a second, his fingertips dig into my skin. Sampson clears his throat before telling me that if Raniero wanted me to know what he did, he'd tell me.

I sigh with frustration when I'm forced back into my prison. I have everything a woman could want in here: food, drinks, books, a television, a soft bed, a bathroom, clothes, and more. But the only thing I really want is something I can't have: answers.

I throw myself on the bed dramatically and scream into the high thread count comforter. My anger is muffled in the deep red and black damask pattern.

My father has been an asshole for as long as I can remember. He's pissed off everyone from state officials to drug dealers on the streets. He's worked at every station in this county and the one next door, but it was only when he started at the Manhattan office that he started working his way up the leadership ladder.

His actions have gotten me in trouble more than once, but this is the first time they've threatened my life. I've been cornered by gangs that he arrested and beaten up by girls' moms he took to jail for selling prescription pills, but they never did more than make a few threats and leave a few bruises.

Whatever my father did to Raniero must have been bad because it's rare that a traffic ticket facilitates this kind of reaction from a man. What did Grant do to piss off Raniero? And why? If he has enough money to have a mansion overlooking the lake, then why did my father fuck with him?

I roll over on the bed and stare up at the ceiling of my new home. I know that it could be worse, but what if Raniero is telling the truth? What if he really plans to get me pregnant, marry me, and keep me here forever?

The little voice in my head tells me that I could do worse than a rich, handsome man with a big dick.

"A big dick I don't know what to do with," I mumble in response even though the voice is only in my head. Who's going to tell the big bad kidnapper that my mouth wasn't the only unpenetrated hole at dinner tonight?

When I was in high school, I didn't have time for

boyfriends. I was busy fending off my father's abusive attacks and keeping my P.E. teacher from seeing the bruises. I learned early on that reporting my dad would only get me into more trouble. He convinced my junior high guidance counselor that I was acting out over the loss of my mother and that I was giving myself those beatings. I couldn't imagine what he'd do if I tried to confide in the high school nurse.

As I got older, I was too busy fighting to stay off the streets and keep my tent from being broken into. I didn't have time for relationships when the only place I could bring a man back to was a friend's couch. I used dating apps to get free dinners from time to time, but nothing ever progressed past a couple of kisses.

When Raniero wants more than a few mouth hugs, who's going to be the one to tell him that I'm untouched goods?

RANIERO

I spent half the night going back through the Jackson family files.

I read through the medical reports that Grant submitted to the police department. He's had high blood pressure for the last five years, but otherwise, he's in peak physical condition. I obtained his annual reviews from last year to the year he first started as a cop. His superiors have always had a high opinion of him, even higher when his violent streak led to drug busts that the station had spent years trying to uncover.

Ares Jackson, the oldest twin by three minutes, was only ever close to his brother. There are very few pictures of him and Calliope over the years. And once he moved to New York, he cut off all contact with his father and younger sister. It made me wonder if Grant had been a little heavy-handed on Ares as well, but with no filed reports, there was no telling. He married the first woman he met and started popping out kids a year later.

Apollo followed his brother to New York but he's kept in contact with the family since his move. He and his wife go over to Ares' every Sunday night for dinner. They work in the high-powered business of finance, but Ares is a Financial Analyst while Apollo is a Financial Operations Manager. Apollo calls Calliope every few weeks to check in and she lies to him about her whereabouts and what she's doing with her life. He texts his dad weekly and the two often chat about the silly things that happen in their perspective lines of work.

Calliope's folder is both the slimmest and the most interesting. She didn't go to college or leave the little apple like her brothers. Her criminal past probably prohibited her from getting the degree she wanted, but also, so did running away from home. Grant happily paid for the twin's bachelor degrees, but the second Calliope stepped out the front door and didn't look back, he cut her off. He was nice enough to seal her youth record, but that didn't stop him from hunting her down on the homeless streets of Manhattan to arrest her for minor infractions.

I knew their reports forward and backward. My men spent weeks gathering intel about the Jackson family and I spent weeks devouring it like a five-course meal at a Michelin-star restaurant. But after my explosion in the dining room, I needed to make sure I hadn't missed something.

By the time morning rolls around, I've had four hours of sleep and I'm in desperate need of a coffee with three shots of espresso if I'm going to make it through the day.

"Good morning, Mr. Valenti," the morning cook greets with a smile. She's a nice woman with two kids at home. Her husband used to be in my service, but he passed a few years ago in the line of duty. I offered her everything from riches to a place to live, but she was happy enough to take a job cooking for me. I pay her an exorbitant fee to make up for her loss and she treats me like one of her sons. "Sampson told me you have a guest staying with us. Do they have any allergies?"

Apollo Jackson is allergic to strawberries. Ares is allergic to shellfish. Calliope is allergy-free. "No, Grace, not that I'm aware of."

She sets down a plate of freshly made waffles

before giving me a pat on the shoulder. "Let me know if that changes, okay?" Then she absentmindedly starts humming as she returns to the kitchen.

I could survive without the staff I employ to care for my home, but my life would be significantly harder. My parents created lifelong wealth for themselves and their kids before leaving me their home and returning to Italy. I use some of that money to give jobs to old friends and people in need. If I would have run across Calliope on the streets and thought she needed a job, I would have offered her one.

Grant Jackson thinks I'm a bad person because the things the Valenti family does aren't completely legal. But I don't see him at elementary school fundraisers or golf tournaments that benefit underprivileged children. He isn't the one keeping his family members afloat with loans that he never expects to be paid back. He doesn't give poor people jobs, keep them off the streets, and help them make a better life for themselves.

I might have bludgeoned a man to death once or twice, but I protect the people that I love.

Sampson enters the dining room with Calliope in his grasp. He's holding onto her arm so tightly that when he releases her, there are white pinpricks from where his fingers were just holding her. "She's very inquisitive," he informs me with a shrug as if he can read the question on my face. "I suspect she's gathering information to plot an escape."

Calliope turns to glare at him as she rubs her arm where his hand once was. "I am not!" She rebuts. "I'm just trying to figure out why I'm here." Today she's wearing a pair of soft, figure-hugging black pants and a red shirt with a fitted bust and an empire waist. Her hair is pulled back into a sleek ponytail.

"I'll take care of it, Sampson. Thanks for your help." I usher her forward and she looks at the floor for a second before hesitantly taking a step in my direction. "You can sit in your own chair," I tell her with a careless wave toward the place setting beside me.

I'm not going to make her crawl around forever. You can call me a nice guy if you want, but frankly, I don't want her to fuck up her knees. I'm going to want to see her on them again and I don't want it to be an uncomfortable experience.

Calliope looks at me and then at the empty seat beside me before finally stepping forward. "Thank you," she mumbles. When she grabs the chair to pull it out, I notice that her nails are chewed to the quick and the skin is torn into ragged strips.

"There are bandaids under the bathroom sink if you need them," I offer gently. I want to reach out and grab her hand, kiss away the pain she holds in her bad habits. But I gesture toward the table instead. "Help yourself."

She hides her torn fingers in the ball of her fist. "Do you have any syrup?" Calliope asks between gritted teeth.

Just then, Grace comes out of the kitchen with a tray full of offerings. There's a bowl full of butter and two others filled to the brim with jelly. She has warm maple syrup in a container that you can see the steam coming off of and next to it is a little bear full of honey. "Forgot about these," she says with a smile as she sets it down on the table, "the maple syrup was still heating. Welcome, miss." Grace nods her head politely at Calliope. I can tell she's curious about what to call our new guest, but Grace doesn't ask in front of her. She knows that I'll tell her when it's needed.

As Grace returns to the kitchen, Calliope is already grabbing the butter and syrup off the tray. She has a waffle on her plate and she's slathering it in butter like she hasn't eaten in a week.

I sip my coffee and watch her in delight. Despite last night's carnal display, she doesn't seem at all bothered to be in my presence. I thought she might be a little put off to see me this morning, but she's more annoyed that I called out her chewed-up fingernails than being around me.

"Your father tried to pin a murder on me." I knew she would have questions; it's my duty to answer them.

Calliope drops her fork. Slowly, she turns her head toward me. "He *what?*" She asks sharply.

I've had run-ins with Police Chief Grant Jackson since he arrived at the Manhattan police department. He's always been a pain in my ass. I don't know what the previous cops told him about the Valenti family, but he's had a vendetta against us since the day he showed up.

He pulled me over for having a tail light out *while* I was on the way to get a new one. He tried to flip the members of my family against me. He arrested me for jaywalking once. None of his charges stuck, but that didn't stop him from trying his damnedest to ruin not just my day, but my entire life.

"I belong to an important family in Manhattan," I explain to Calliope. "While we are incredibly philanthropic, there are others in town that see us as predatory."

"The Valentis," Calliope snaps her fingers together in recognition. "I thought Raniero was a strange name."

I glare at her and bark back, "Because Calliope is so normal." This shuts her up immediately. "The point here is that *your* father has been running a smear campaign against me for over a decade. When someone was beaten to death in an alley a few months ago, he had me hauled in for questioning despite having a clear alibi for the night in question."

Calliope snorts as her eyes return to her plate. "Yeah, that's my dad for ya," she says with a roll of her eyes. She grabs her knife and starts cutting into her waffle.

"That was the last straw for me. He threatened to come after everyone related to me, even tangentially so. Which means people like Grace, who only cook and do some light kitchen clean up for me, are constantly being pulled over for minor traffic violations or just because an officer wants to fuck with me." Last month Grace went through a yellow light just as it turned and she was given a ticket. I paid it before she was sent a bill, but I shouldn't have had to.

"Grant has made it his life's mission to give me hell, so I decided to give it right back to him. What would cut him off at the knees?" I look Calliope up and down as she shoves a forkful of waffle into her mouth. "Having to regard me as family. That's where you come in."

She nearly chokes on her food. Calliope is laughing as she tries to chew and swallow what's in her mouth. "You thought you'd use me to get back at my father?" She snorts again in an unattractive manner. "You wasted your time then. I ran away years ago and he hasn't given two shits about me since. Unless he found me on the streets, of course," Calliope mumbles. "Then he's all too happy to scoop me up and take me to jail for the night for vagrancy."

And somehow *I'm* the bad guy. "Not anymore." I ball my hands into fists and have to talk myself off a ledge. I half consider driving down to the police station right now and giving Chief Jackson a piece of my mind. But I'm aiming to get my revenge, not immediate but underwhelming gratification for knocking his teeth in. I want to see him squirm for the rest of his life the way he's trying to make me. "You'll never be homeless again, Calliope."

She isn't phased by the promise. Instead, she takes a couple more bites before responding to me. "All I've done is trade one prison for another, Raniero. I was finally making something of myself before you came along. I might have endured another cycle of poverty eventually, but maybe I wouldn't have. Maybe I would have been fine on my own."

It's her first outburst since I pulled out the gun at her open house. It isn't much, but it shows me that she has a fighting spirit. She had been barely scraping by for years, but Calliope still believed that she would change her fortunes one day. "Maybe," I agree with her carefully, "but now you don't have to find out. You are mine now, Calliope, and I will do whatever I want with my property. Including breed it, marry it, and use it for revenge."

8

CALLIOPE

Begrudgingly I must admit that the grounds are stunning. I looked out my bedroom window for a while yesterday while waiting for dinner to roll around and I was given an ample view of the gardens. From up above, I could see that the carefully planted flowers and bushes formed a maze that lead to a water fountain in the center. A marble statue stood proudly, water gushing from its teats. It was a reminder of fertility.

Since I was on the side of the house that faced away from the lake, Raniero offered to take me on a walk after breakfast. If I had known what was going to happen, I would have worn something more suited for the sun. Instead, I roasted alive under the ubiquitous rays of the heat on my black pants.

Unfortunately, humiliation was back on the table. Before we left the mansion, Raniero stopped me at the front door to put a collar around my neck. It fit snugly against my throat and had a metal ring that he positioned just under my chin. A few moments later, I found out why.

"I don't want to risk you running away," he said with a smile as he clipped a leash to the ring. "Now if you try, I'll be able to stop you in your tracks."

It was bad enough that he'd made me crawl on my hands and knees the night before. Like a dog, he fed me table scraps as I knelt at his side. He continues that treatment today, walking me like a bitch in heat.

But it is nice to be outside. The windows in my bedroom don't open; I tried to get through them last night. I might have been on the second floor, but I would have risked a broken leg to escape. *But escape back to what?* The little voice in my head asks. And I know that she's right. I could return home if I wanted, but I wouldn't be returning to much. An apartment with minimal furniture and more food than clothes. A friendless existence because I couldn't afford to go bar hopping or wine tasting with my coworkers. Wondering when the other shoe was going to drop and I was going to lose it all.

"—and then we'll get married," Raniero says, pulling me out of my trance.

My head snaps to the side to look at him with a frown pulling across my features. "What did you say?"

He tuts his tongue at me and pulls on the thin, black leash attached to my collar. If I tried to escape, it wouldn't stop me, but it would certainly slow me down. "Pay attention when I speak to you, Calliope."

I guess I should be thankful that he hasn't raised a fist at me yet. Or taken the belt off of his pants and started beating me across the back with it. My father did both when I was younger. His actions drove me to rebellion and then, ultimately, to running away. "Sorry," I mumble my apology to Raniero, "I won't do it again."

His face softens and he gives my leash some slack. I use it to walk a step ahead of him while taking in the view. The lake is a few hundred yards ahead, but we'll never reach it. Instead, a gate has been erected around the edge of the property. Black metal bars stand ten feet tall with enough space to allow my arm through but nothing else.

"My grandparents bought this land over a century ago." Raniero comes up to stand beside me when I stop walking. As I glance over at him, I notice that his facial hair is more gray than black, a sign of aging. "They passed it on to my parents and they built a home here. I've always lived here," he says with a hint of nostalgia in his tone. "My brothers and I grew up throwing rocks at the lake's shore and playing tag in the garden. Mother hated it, but she never stopped us."

When you're in a hostage situation and the kidnapper has a gun to your head, you're supposed to make yourself memorable. You recite facts about your life like how many kids you have at home and what you do for a living. You make yourself someone that the kidnapper can't forget because they'll be less inclined to kill you.

Though I'm not holding a gun to Raniero's head, he seems to be parceling me information as if I were, as if to endear himself to me. He seems less like the dark, dangerous figure that kidnapped me on a Sunday afternoon and more like a human being. It makes this feel more like a date than what it truly is.

"Where are your parents now?" I ask after a few moments. I shouldn't. I should keep my mouth shut and pretend not to hear him. The less I know about Raniero Valenti, the more I can hate him. But a few of my father's well-intentioned life lessons, albeit executed poorly, sunk in over the years. I am respectful to a T, always.

Raniero turns to face me and I catch a glimpse of his dark, beautiful eyes. A flicker of intimacy mixes with the cruelty in his gaze. "A few years ago they decided to move back to Italy. My mother was originally from Sicily and my father's parents were from a neighboring village. Though he'd lived in the states all his life, he wanted to give my mother the retirement that she deserved. Because he loved her so much."

I never should have asked. Just the way that he looks at me tells me everything I need to be afraid of. Raniero's eyes say that he would do the same for me if we got to that point one day and it makes it hard for me to look at him.

I turn away and stare at the fence, suddenly wondering what it would take to scale it. There is a bar that runs perpendicular across the bottom hovering five inches above the ground. Another bar mimics its pattern across the top. I'm not a tall woman, I'm barely half the size of the fence, but it wouldn't take much to grab the top bar and hoist myself aloft. I'm not in terrible shape and I certainly don't have a lot of weight to carry with me. Living off of nothing some days and just a little more on others has left me with a fast metabolism and a thin figure.

"Don't think about it." Raniero wraps the leash around his fist and pulls it taut. The tugging of my collar forces me toward him. "My parents built this fence to keep people out. There's a thin strand across the top bar," he gestures with his head. "The second you grab it, you'll be electrocuted. Not enough to kill you, but enough to make you wish you were dead."

A shiver races down my spine. I already wish I wasn't here while simultaneously wondering how I got to be so lucky. I can't imagine what it would be like to touch that electric wire and get the shock of a lifetime.

"Half this town thinks we're the bad guys. Teenagers try to break in. Cops try to scour our grounds when we aren't home. Our enemies come here searching for a way to weaken us." Raniero stares at the black fence that seems to go on forever. It curves around the property, narrowly obstructing the view of the lake. "The fence isn't meant to keep you in, it's meant to keep the real bad guys out."

Does he know how crazy that sounds? "Those bad guys didn't kidnap me in broad daylight," I mumble more to myself than to him.

Raniero reaches up to grab my chin. Just like last night, he forces me to stare at him. The intimacy from earlier has disappeared and is replaced with anger. "No, they would have done worse to you. If Grant Jackson had threatened their families, they would have killed you in broad daylight and sent the video to your father. They wouldn't have done their research. They wouldn't have figured out the most painful way to wound him. They would have shot first and asked questions later."

All my life I thought that my father's job protected me from the worst of humankind. In actuality, it revealed it to me in its truest form.

"I am doing you a favor, Calliope. I am saving you from what can happen to you if your father gets you behind bars *again*. I am saving you from living on the streets *again*. I am saving you from worse men than me finding you and doing unspeakable things to you." He releases my face with a shove disparate from his fist tugging on the leash. "You're a beautiful girl, Calliope, and I will spend the rest of my life ensuring that you stay that way. So don't think about escaping and running back to your old life. You are mine now and soon you will bear my children and my name."

"What about love?" I cut him off with a glare. "What about being with someone you care about?"

Raniero gives me a cold, cruel smile that speaks to the depths of his depravity. "I've been watching you for weeks. I know the deodorant you use. You know the kind, the clear Secret with lavender and vanilla. I know what your body smells like after a hard day's work." He tugs the leash tighter until I'm wincing as I step into him once more. There is no space between our bodies, just clothes keeping us separated.

"Once when I was in your apartment, I found a pair of your panties lying on the floor. I brought those to my nose and inhaled your scent. I knew right then and there that there was no one else in this world for me. You made me hard and you weren't even in the room." He's so close that I can feel his warm breath on my face. "I love you in the strangest sense of the word. I love you like a man loves something he's obsessed with. And one day, you will love me, too."

A trickle of sweat beads on my back and slithers down my spine. I am horrified and aroused. But mostly, I'm terrified.

If this is a man that can break into my apartment, steal my clothes, and learn everything about me down to the deodorant that I wear, then what kind of person am I dealing with? Should I fight for my freedom or let him steamroll me like he is intending to do?

Do I even have a choice?

9

RANIERO

The first five days were the hardest. Christopher Ray came to the house a few hours after I'd kidnapped Calliope from the house. He wanted to ensure the realtor had locked everything up and that nothing was missing. Instead, he found her car still in the driveway and her purse on the kitchen counter. Assuming the worst, he called the cops.

Chief Jackson was deliberately directed elsewhere as the officers thought it best not to inform him just yet that his daughter had gone missing. Not to mention they told Christopher that a police report couldn't be filed until she'd been gone for twenty-four hours anyway. "I'm not filing a report or nothing," Christopher told the police. "I'm just saying that my realtor was here earlier today and now she's not. Her stuff is here though and that's concerning."

Twenty-four hours later on the dot, a police report was filed by Chief Jackson. His officers realized that they needed to inform him of what was happening. Since Calliope's real estate brokerage hadn't heard from her, they needed Grant's help locating her. All Grant could do was drop by her apartment and demand that she open the door. When she didn't, he spent the rest of the night pacing around his living room and screaming at his girlfriend.

I had a man watching from the street and he said that Grant wasn't even upset that his daughter was missing. The Chief of Police was angry that she was causing a scene that involved him.

The police searched the Ray residence for fingerprints. They found mine mixed among dozens of others and we were all brought into the station for questioning.

"I know you did it," Grant snarled at me from across the interrogation table. It was the second time this year that I'd been hauled into the police station and it was getting tiresome.

"Did what?" I sounded bored because I was.

Grant didn't have anything on me. He couldn't prove if I'd been at the open house because Christopher Ray was forced to inform the police that we were acquaintances. His wife had to come forward and say that she'd invited me over a few weeks before. They were my alibi.

"You have my daughter, don't you? You said you'd hurt my family," he accused.

But I shook my head no and crossed my arms over my chest. "No, I said I didn't *have* to hurt your family. Besides, maybe your daughter was just tired of putting up with your bullshit. I hear you're a wife-beater, Chief Jackson. I bet if I asked her, she'd tell me that you beat her, too."

His face exploded with embarrassment and rage. He slammed his fists down on the table for only a second before grabbing the metal chair and flinging it at the wall. "You fucking Italian thug. If I find out you took my daughter, I swear to God, I'll—"

"—what?" I cut him off. "You'll do what? You weren't even close. Nobody is going to believe that you're leading the missing person hunt when you arrested her just two years ago for some bullshit jaywalking charge." I stood up with all the conviction of a wrongly accused man and demanded to be released. "Come back when you have some proof, Jackson. I'm getting sick of spending my afternoons with you."

But everything was calming down, or at least I assumed it was. Nobody had called me in twenty-four hours and one meeting with the editor of the newspaper kept my name out of the press. I wasn't on trial for anything; I wasn't even a suspect anymore. Life was easy peasy with my stolen goods locked upstairs.

I needed a break from the life of a kidnapper and decided to make a trip into town. My house on the lake was only twenty minutes from the heart of Manhattan, but it made for a nice little drive. I had decided to have lunch with a couple of my brothers at a tap house that served bar food and craft beers.

Mateo was already at Tallgrass when I arrived. He had chosen a spot on the roof away from the other guests. A storm cloud hung off in the distance and there was rain on the forecast for later in the day, but for now, we enjoyed the sun that we could. "They got chorizo crab dip," Mateo announces as I walk up. He flips over the paper menu while shaking his head in awe. "Fucking chorizo and crab, Nero." Mateo had a flight of beers in front of him. Four mini glasses were filled from the lightest pale straw pilsner to the darkest stout on tap.

"Any of those good?" I ask as I sit down.

He grabs one of the beers in the center and shrugs. "A lot of IPAs," he says as if that's an explanation. But a minute later he chugs the whole thing like it's a shot.

"I think I'll settle for a Bloody Mary." I grab the menu on the table and glance over it. Since we're on the roof, our selections are limited. You can't get soup when the waitress has to walk up three flights of stairs to get it to you.

Luca arrives a few moments later with his eyes glued to his phone. His fingers tap furiously on the screen and without looking up, he dodges other diners, waiters, and planter boxes on his way over to us on the other side of the roof. "I gotta town council meeting in forty-eight minutes," he announces as he sits down. "Is that the Predator doppelbock? I want one." He immediately starts to look around for a waitress, raising his hand to get some attention.

"Jesus," I swear at him, "you're so embarrassing to be with. And why are you drinking before a town council meeting?"

He ignores me long enough to order a pint of the Predator and finish his text message. Luca slams the phone down on the table with impressive force and it draws the eyes of everyone else on the rooftop. Thankfully, he has a case on his phone or else I swear the glass backing would have shattered. "*Because* it helps me deal with people like you," Luca says with a charming smile.

Luca, for reasons that escape the rest of the family, is heavily involved with the politics of Manhattan. A year ago he managed to worm his way onto the City Commission and he's absolutely certain that he'll be Mayor in two years. He likes to say that he's going to run for President one day, but the rest of us know that won't be possible. You don't have to look too hard to find out a few of Luca Valenti's dirty secrets.

"Anyway," Luca taps his fingers on the table aggressively impatient. "Why are we here? What do you want?'

He's a busy man, and I shouldn't waste his time, but Luca sometimes rubs me the wrong way. "I was thinking of repainting the house and I wanted your opinion on the colors."

Luca's jaw drops. I swear I see my life flash before his eyes as he considers leaping across this table to choke me out.

"Relax," I roll my eyes before he lets his baser instincts win, "it's more serious than that."

Mateo snorts when Luca lets out a sigh of frustration and petulantly throws himself back in the chair. "Forgive me for putting the cart before the horse, but you wouldn't be calling us here about the Jackson kidnapping case, would you?" He shrugs his shoulders with I grin. "I know you've had problems with that officer."

"*I've* had problems with the Chief of Police," Luca corrects his older brother. "I half considered bringing it up to the Commission to have him removed. If he tickets my car for being two minutes over the three-hour parking limit *one more time*," he threatens.

I raise my hand to silence him. Luca is the middle child of the five Valenti boys and he's forever trying to make himself more important. I suspect sometimes that that's why he went against the family's reputation to become a political figure in town. The rest of the Valentis are criminals and he's an upstanding City Commissioner with a bright future. Blah, blah, blah. Middle child shit. "He's a pain in the ass, Luc, but I'm taking care of it."

Mateo grabs another glass of beer from his flight and sips half of it in one gulp. "Oh, yeah? By kidnapping his daughter? What are you going to do with her, Nero? Dangle her as bait? Newsflash: the rest of us can do our research, too. She and daddy *piece of shit* aren't even close."

I don't know why he didn't call me earlier in the week if he assumed that I was behind Calliope's kidnapping. We could have resolved this over the phone like men instead of duking it out over IPAs and chorizo crab dip. "Yeah, thanks, Sherlock, I figured that one out for myself."

The server arrives with Luca's pint and drops it off. We quickly rattle off our orders with minimal questions before she turns on her heels and leaves mumbling under her breath.

"She's gotta nice ass." Luca can't tear his eyes off of her even when the bartender catches him looking. I snap my fingers at him to get his attention; instead, he bites my head off. "Yo, fucking do it again, Raniero. Snap at me like I'm a dog one more time. I fucking dare you."

This is why the family doesn't get together much anymore. Luca has anger management problems and a schedule so jam-packed that he barely had forty-eight minutes to squeeze us in for lunch. And when he does manage to see us, he reverts back to his place in the Valenti family and stirs the shit for fun.

I ignore him as best as I can. I know we just placed our orders, but if my burger doesn't get here soon, a mixture of hunger and frustration will force me to haul off and hit my brother. "Yes, I kidnapped Calliope Jackson. After that incident where he tried to frame me," I shake my head just remembering it, "and then threatened my family, I was forced to do what I had to do to protect our family."

Mateo and Luca exchange a look between the two of them. Wisely, Mateo is the one that chooses to speak first. "You decided to protect our family by pissing off the single legal entity that can take us down?"

I would have run this decision past my brothers, all four of them, if I thought that they needed to know about it before it happened. Instead, I ran it past my Consigliere, Gianluca. He had some reservations and we talked those through like adults. He didn't question me like he was undermining my decisions—unlike Mateo, whose tone puts me on the defensive. "He needs to be taught a lesson. The other day he called me a fucking Italian thug."

It's Luca's turn to snort in derision as he checks

his watch and takes a healthy gulp from his pint glass. "Someone calls you a bad name and you decide to commit a felony?"

"He's going to be calling me son-in-law soon," I return with a glare.

Their eyebrows raise at the same time, curiosity highlighting their features. "Come again?" Mateo asks.

I sit back in my chair and finally take a deep breath. My brothers might give me shit for the choices I make, but they're always impressed with my reasoning. When our father left me to run the family's empire, they were hesitant that I'd make a good leader. But I've shown them time and time again that the Valenti family isn't just a name with a violent past. I brought us into the twenty-first century. "I kidnapped Calliope to marry her and knock her up. Once the Jackson name is tied to ours, the Chief won't be so quick to tear us down."

"You're going to marry her?" Mateo's nose crinkles in disgust. "She's not very active on social media so maybe her pictures are a little old. But is she even attractive?"

Calliope is 5'2" with a lithe figure. Her tits are the size of teacups. Her hips are delicate and her ass is there, but in baggy enough clothes, you'd never notice it. She isn't like the buxom beauties I've been out with before, but she is alluring in her own way. "Yes," I glare at him. "There's more to her than meets the eye." Like her submission. And the way she looks at me with those bright, vulnerable green eyes.

"I've always wanted to get a girl pregnant." Luca kicks his feet up on the table and looks off into the distance with a curved smile on his face. "Watch her belly swell with my seed. See her tits get fuller and her hips widen. Pregnant women are beautiful."

I'll admit that I agree with him. There's nothing better than the glow of pregnancy on a woman's face. "That'll come after the wedding," I tell him with a shrug. "And the wedding won't happen until after she's broken. I have to be able to trust her and right now I'm certain that if given the chance, she'd run away."

Luca only laughs. It's enough to draw attention back to us once more. This time it's followed by frowns and glares from the other diners. "Break her by breaking her in, Nero. Fill her pussy good, knock her up, and then invite Chief fucking Jackson to your shotgun wedding. I *guarantee* he'll be less of a prick when he finds out that you cream-pied his daughter."

I hadn't thought about getting her pregnant first. That idea has some merit. "You might be onto something, Luca."

He gives me a wink before saying, "And you might be *into* something when you get back home, am I right?"

It's a dirty joke and I can't help but laugh. He's not wrong. After that first night I forced her to blow me, I've been struggling through cold showers while telling myself to back off. Maybe I had the wrong idea.

CALLIOPE

Five days. That's how long I've been locked up in this mansion. Made to eat all of my meals with Raniero and listen to him wax poetically about the life we're going to lead after we're married. I go between anger and hope; torn between excitement and fear.

If Raniero allowed me to roam freely, perhaps I'd have more time to get to know him. But Sampson drops by my room every few hours to check on me and he's evasive when I ask for his boss. *Would* I have more time to get to know Raniero? Or is he leaving during the hours that he's not with me?

Our time spent together is strained. He refuses to take back the collar he placed around my neck and threatened me if I removed it. The leather is soft against my skin, but what it represents makes my stomach churn.

I only take it off to shower and in those few minutes, I feel like myself again. With the waterfall showerhead bathing me in freedom, I close my eyes and pretend I'm anywhere except this ornate, comfortable prison.

The little voice in my head is constantly reminding me that this is better than the streets. The fact that I can control the air conditioning is better than roasting alive under the Kansas sun while humidity sucks every drop of hydration from my body. But the little voice goes suspiciously dormant when I ask how I'm supposed to enjoy my surroundings when they're also the walls keeping me captive.

If I'm being honest, and I'm only honest with myself in the middle of the night when the little voice is asleep, this isn't that bad. Raniero feeds me and takes care of me. Like the dog that I am to him, he walks me every day. The thin, strappy leash that he keeps wrapped around his fist has become the stuff of my nightmares. Once, just a couple of days before, we walked the grounds during sunset and he held me while we stood in front of the garden.

I could almost forget that he pulled a gun on me

and forced me into his car. I could almost forget that first night that he made me crawl on my hands and knees and sit by his side like a begging puppy. I could almost forget the taste of his spunk on my tongue when he came in my mouth.

Almost.

With his strong arms wrapped around my waist, I almost felt safe. Until he slapped the thin leather leash against the palm of his hand and chuckled in my ear. "I wonder if it would make the same sound on your ass."

A shiver raced down my spine and a lump formed in my throat. He wanted to hit me. He wanted to hurt me. He wanted to—

"Pain can be pleasurable," he added a few seconds later as if he could read my thoughts. "In fact, if done right, you can even orgasm from it."

I wiggled out of his grasp and almost fell into the fountain. As I was twisting and turning trying to escape from his sensual whispers, the back of my leg buckled against the concrete bench that encircled the fountain. I flailed backward until Raniero's grip on the leash tugged me forward into his arms.

Trapped once more, heart racing, I looked up at him. "Come, little dove," he smirked, "let's go to bed."

I was afraid of what he meant by those words. Every step we took back toward his ostentatious mansion filled me with dread. Was he going to touch me when we got back to my room? Was he going to strip me down and force me to my knees again? And why was the little voice in my head suddenly cheering him on?

But all Raniero did was press his lips to mine before locking me in my cozy prison cell. "You'll come to crave me one day, like water on a hot day. And I'll always be around to quench your thirst."

Today my lunch was served to me by Sampson. I readied myself to go downstairs to eat with Raniero, but I was met by his bodyguard at our usual dining time. "A summer salad, miss." He brings the tray into my room and sets it down on the desk near the door. "And a delicious butternut squash soup." He leaves without telling me why I'm eating alone.

The cook, Grace, asked me a few nights ago what my dining preferences were. I looked at Raniero as if silently asking for permission to answer her. He nodded his head with a benevolent smile and I told her what I knew. No, I'd never had seafood. Yes, I loved sweets. I had no allergies. I was willing to try anything once. I hated mayonnaise.

The salad she made for me today looks divine. There are bits of grilled chicken, strawberries, blueberries, and pecans doled out among the lettuce. A delicious poppy seed dressing with just a hint of sweetness coats everything. It's simple and fresh and it tastes amazing.

The butternut squash soup is just as good. Toward the end of the bowl, I find myself picking it up and clanking my spoon against the ceramic to get out every last drop. The tray came with a snack size amount of buttery crackers, but I store them in my closet pantry for later, too stuffed to eat them now.

I waste the rest of the afternoon. Right after lunch, I take an hour-long nap. When Raniero still hasn't arrived, I retire to the bathroom where I fill the tub with bubbles and sink down to my nose. You could say that I'm pampered here, but I am still a captive.

Once I feel clean and can't stand the heat of the bath any longer, I dry off and plant myself on the window ledge with a book. A few minutes pass and the pages practically turn themselves as I'm pulled into a world of politics, lust, and intrigue. Then the door opens and I'm jarred from my place.

After missing lunch and leaving me to spend the afternoon entertaining myself, Raniero stands in the door frame with just a pair of jeans hanging around his hips. "Just what a man wants to come home to," he says with a lascivious grin.

I try to tear my eyes off his body but it's hopeless. What he's done doesn't matter when he looks like that. A patch of sparse curls on his chest, somehow emphasizing the muscles beneath. Hard, shapely abs line his stomach. There's a prominent freckle above his right hip bone that begs me to run my fingers across it. "Raniero," I try to say his name confidently, but it comes out in a half-stuttered mess.

He steps through the door and shoves it closed behind him. The wood makes a cracking sound beneath the weight. "Calliope," he mimics, his voice sounding more at ease than mine.

I dog-ear the page of the book I'm on and set it in front of me on the windowsill. "Did you have a good lunch?" I could tell him about my day, but what's there to say? Since I saw him at breakfast, I've done precious little.

Raniero doesn't answer me. Instead, he crosses the room until he's standing next to me. He stares down at me with his dark, forbidden gaze and waits for me to look up at him. He's quiet and it makes my heart pound in my chest.

When I finally gather the courage to look up at him, he licks his bottom lip. Then Raniero puts his hand out to me and I know that I have no choice but to take it. "That's a good girl," he praises as he pulls me to my feet. "Do you know that I can smell your arousal?" He takes me in his arms. "There's a trickle of sweat between your breasts that tells me you're afraid of what that means, but don't be alarmed, little dove. I only mean to make you feel very, *very* good."

I open my mouth to protest and he cuts me off with a kiss. I'm taken aback as he forces his tongue into my mouth. He explores me in the most intimate way and it leaves me breathless.

Raniero's hands chart a new course over my curves. He drags his fingers over a sensitive patch of skin near my hip and it causes me to shudder. All the while, he keeps me trapped between his body and the windowsill. There is nowhere for me to go; I am forced to submit to his desires.

I really do forget all the bad things he's done this time. When he pulls his lips away from mine, it's only to reposition them on my jawline. He slips lower and lower with each passing second as he trails kisses down my neck. I bite my bottom lip and try to hold onto my sanity, but it feels like it's slipping through my fingers.

"Are you on birth control?" He mumbles against my collarbone.

My stomach twists into knots and I find myself reaching forward to grab onto him. It isn't out of lust, it's to keep myself from falling backward. "I-I-I," I stutter, trying to push him away or pull myself back, whichever will put some distance between the two of us.

But Raniero only holds me tighter and grinds his body into mine. His cock creates an impressive bulge in his jeans as it presses against my stomach. "Ah, ah, ah," his smile presses against my throat, "I asked you a question."

My heart feels like it's going to beat right out of my chest. "No," I respond quietly.

His grip tightens for a second in delight. "Perfect," Raniero chuckles. "I want to see your belly swell with my seed as soon as possible."

A scream of admissions echoes through my head. *I've never had sex before. I don't know how to be a mom. I barely know you.* But they are quashed by his quickness. I never get a chance to put a voice to my truths before he's tugging at the hem of my shirt and baring me in front of him.

I didn't put a bra on after getting out of the bathtub because I didn't expect to see Raniero until dinner. This gives him an ample view of my breasts and I reach up to cover them with crossed arms.

He's quick to grab my forearms and stop me. "I don't want you to hide from me, Calliope." An edge to his tone tells me that this isn't a joke. "You are my perfect, untouched princess and I want to see all of you."

I have to turn my head to keep from looking at him. My face is filled with shame when he brings a hand up to my chest and runs his thumb across my nipple. It's almost enough to make me cry when the sensation causes the skin to pebble.

"You're turned on by me," he asserts.

I can't stop my body from reacting. Raniero is strong and attractive and he touches me like a master handling a prized horse. "I can't help my reactions," I mutter under my breath.

He grabs my chin and tilts it up so that I'm forced to look at him. "I'm not going to hurt you, Calliope. I need you to know that."

"You kidnapped me. You are holding me hostage." I frown.

Raniero shrugs. "That was all necessary. I needed you so that I could teach your father a lesson."

"I struggle to understand what my father's transgressions have to do with me." I rip my chin out of his hand and try to push past him, but he only allows me to go so far before grabbing my wrist and holding me in place. "Why me?" I glare back at him.

Once again his shoulders make a little up-and-down motion. Raniero's face is passive when he tells me that it's complicated. "When I first saw your picture, I was drawn to you. I could have put it down and gone after your brothers instead, or your father's girlfriend, but the more I found out about you, the harder it was to leave you alone." His eyebrows crease as he looks at me. "Your father hated you. He hurt you and he ruined your life. He *enjoyed* ruining your life. I thought we'd bond over shoveling a heap of shit on top of his head for once."

It isn't romantic. This whole situation will make me feel icky when I think about it later.

I'm standing shirtless before the man that kidnapped me for revenge. He makes me feel like a dog half the time and the other half he ignores me. He talks about our future together like it's set in stone.

There's no reason for me to give in to him. I can't fathom why I'd let him fuck me. But I do.

Sometimes you find solace in the most unlikely of places. Like the very man that turned your life upside down.

11

RANIERO

When Calliope steps toward me and stands on her toes, she isn't tall enough to kiss me. I do her the service of bending my head just a few inches to read her mouth.

I don't know what changed within her in those few moments, but it's enough to change her entire attitude. I want to devour her whole, but now she kisses me like she's hungry, too.

We press our naked torsos together and it's an awkward shuffle to the bed. But when the back of her knees hit the edge, they buckle and send her sailing backward. Calliope lands on the comforter with an indiscernible thump.

Seeing her from this angle, I catch sight of the goosebumps covering her arms. There is a tremor in her thigh muscle as it flexes tight and releases over and over again. Her nipples form tiny little points at the end of her breasts.

This is the moment where I could be a good guy. I could grab her shirt off the floor and have her put it back on. We could walk across the grounds until my lust for her subsides. It would endear her to me and make our wedding night and subsequent marriage easier.

But I've never been the hero of anyone's story; I've always been the villain.

I reach forward to grab the cloth shorts around her waist and start dragging them down her thighs. I carefully watch the look in her eyes as I toss them behind me. She dons a pair of pink panties that sport a wet spot right in her center.

There are all kinds of things that I want to do to this woman. I've fantasized about being inside of her in every room of the house. And yet, the most erotic sight I've ever seen is the spread of her legs after I remove her last stitch of clothing.

The female body is beautiful. The curves, the straight lines, the stretch marks that dapple the skin like battle scars. Calliope has a tuft of hair on her mound, neatly trimmed as if she was expecting company. The dampness of her arousal provides a slick entrance to her center.

As much as I want to take off my jeans and rip through her virginity like the winner of a marathon, I caution myself to be patient.

I run my hands along her thighs, feeling her body like a blind man reading braille for the first time. I memorize the curve of her calf and the stretch of her leg as I bring it over my shoulder. Face settled between her legs, her entire body shakes when I lean forward and drag my tongue over her center. It is the first of many strokes, but the only one that counts. Calliope's legs part a little wider and give me unfettered access to her pussy. She takes a deep breath that scores the room with her desire.

I hold onto her hips as I explore the curves and crevices of her core, but she still bucks when my tongue waffles over her clit. A stifled moan escapes her lips and when I look up, I see her biting a clenched fist.

I don't want her to hold back. I don't want to see her keeping her cries to herself. I beat my tongue down on her sensitive little button until she's forced to grab onto the blankets while grinding her pussy against my face. The stubble on my chin is coated in her juices as she moves this way and that to get the pressure she needs.

My life has been filled with beautiful women. Some were with me because they wanted to be and others indulged in my pleasures in hopes of finding a way to benefit from my attention. Calliope is the first to land in my bed that didn't come by her own wishes.

That's why I make her scream when she comes. She'll be my wife one day and I want her to remember this moment fondly. I don't want her to think I took her virginity; I want her to believe that she willingly gave it to me in exchange for pleasure.

Calliope wraps her thighs around my head and squeezes so tight that the world around us ceases to exist. Her pussy trembles with the aftershocks of her orgasm. And right in the center of her belly is a small pool of sweat.

It's difficult to extract myself from this position when I could stay here for days, but she won't impregnate herself. I pull away from her with the scent of her excitement left on my face. I smell her lust and her fear, a heady combination of hormones that create her signature perfume.

While she scrambles to scoot further onto the bed, I slowly undress before her. Belt thrown behind me. Jeans sloughed off on the floor. Boxers flung away in a hurry. Calliope leans against the pillows with wide eyes focused right on my cock.

I palm it in my hand. "Do you see what you do to me?" I ask her as I step toward the bed. "Do you see how hard you make me?"

Calliope gnaws on her bottom lip and shakes her head no. "That won't fit," she whispers. "You can't," she protests.

But it will. And I can. I can fuck her every which way from now until Sunday. "Spread your legs," I order. "I'll show you how perfectly it fits inside of you, baby."

She looks at me as if I just asked her to cut an arm off. "Raniero," Calliope starts to beg, "please."

I climb onto the bed and crawl toward her. When I'm positioned over her, one hand on each side of her head, I sweep down to brush my lips against hers. "I said that I wouldn't hurt you, Calliope, and I mean it. Now spread your legs for daddy and let me pop your cherry."

I use my knee to force her thighs apart; Calliope doesn't resist. I position myself at her entrance and feel the slick proof of her arousal on the head of my cock. With my hand gripping my shaft, I drag my tip through her juices until it's soaked and I think I'm about to come all over her pussy. "This might hurt at first," I warn as I start to press my head into her center. "But after a minute or two, it'll start to feel real good, baby. Just trust me."

Whether she trusts me or not, she tentatively nods her head in agreement and lets me continue.

I've deflowered a lot of untouched gardens before and I know that there's no use in wiggling it in little by little. I thrust my hips forward and tear through the veil of her virginity in milliseconds. It takes Calliope by surprise and I'm treated to a squeal of pain. She reaches up to grab my arms and digs her fingernails into my skin. "That's the most pain you'll feel," I reassure her quickly. "And it'll be over in a second." I don't tell her that there might be a little blood, that sometimes when the hymen is torn, it leaves red evidence in its wake.

When the shock on Calliope's face starts to disappear, I allow myself to move inside of her. She repositions her legs in between thrusts, a pained look on her face. But when I grab her thigh and hoist it over my hip, her heel digging into the small of my back, my cock hits just the right spot.

Pleasure blossoms on her features as her jaw drops open and she shuts her eyes. Whether she knows it or not, she's fucking me right back. Her hips move in time with mine and little moans fracture the air.

I grunt as I rut inside of her, thrusting my hips so hard that our skin slaps together when I'm buried to the hilt. Her pussy tightens around me like a turtleneck. The way we fit together is like two puzzle pieces made for one another.

Sweat forms on my brow as I do everything I can to make her orgasm again. Science says they don't do anything to help or deter a woman from getting pregnant, but Calliope will be more amenable if she's coming off a high.

I work her back and forth, left to right, at three different speeds, and I even jackhammer her pussy until she's screaming. She's going to be sore tomorrow when I'm finished with her.

I bet if I flipped her on her belly and fucked her from behind, she'd orgasm with no problem. I could reach around her hip and finger her clit until she couldn't hold back anymore.

But in the end, I don't need all that. As much as I'd like to see her ass jiggle as I pound into her in doggy style, she comes before I get the chance. I feel her muscles contract around me and it sends me over the edge.

My cock coats her walls and forces me to grab

the headboard, fingers tight around the wood as I undulate my hips back and forth. I milk myself inside of her, making sure every last drop of my cum fills her.

"Raniero," she groans, her ineffectual little hands trying to shove me off her, "you should have pulled out."

I don't know why she thought that I would. I've been telling her since I kidnapped her that she was going to have my babies.

I leave my sensitive prick inside of her and rest on my forearms. My body hovers over hers, the heat of our skin-on-skin contact making the sweat on my forehead drip onto her chest. "If I could, I'd stay like this for the rest of the day," I whisper in her ear. "Keep my cum inside of you until my seed implants." I've always wanted to be a father. More than that, I've always wanted a wife walking around my home barefoot and pregnant.

"This pussy is mine now, baby. I'm gonna keep you so full of cum that you'll feel me inside of you even when I'm gone." I wiggle my hips a little, thrusting my seed further into her. "I'm gonna fill you up until your belly is swollen with my child. Then I'll do it again for fun. Just to see my cream pie drip out of your ravaged wet pussy."

Calliope swallows hard. Her fingernails are still dug deep into my biceps and there's a wild look in her eyes. "Stop," she mumbles unconvincingly. "You don't mean that."

I thrust my hips into her one more time, my cock coming back to life. "Tell me what I don't mean again," I threaten. "And I won't just fill your pussy, baby. I'll make sure my cum is dripping out of every one of your holes."

She shudders beneath me but that's when I catch it, the look of excitement. She's afraid, she's been afraid since I kidnapped her, but Calliope can't hide the fact that her libido is titillated by my words. Maybe she doesn't want me to finish inside of her, but something within Calliope is turned on by the idea.

That's the girl that I fuck again. The one that wants to be so full of my jizz that she's a double-stuffed Oreo. I give it to her again until we're both screaming this time. Her fingernails leave marks on my back when I hit her G-spot just right.

Maybe she's not ready to be a mom, but she's ready to get fucked like she is.

12

___

CALLIOPE

Raniero is an animal. He's a god damn fucking monster. And I hate that I like it.

After that first time we had sex, he drew me a bath and said that it would help with my achy muscles. My muscles weren't achy, but I took the bath anyway. It gave me time to think about what had just happened and how my body responded to his. He left the room and locked the door behind him, giving me the privacy to touch myself in memory of what we did. I was ashamed, but I couldn't help but be turned on.

Was it wrong to lust after the man keeping you captive? Was this what they called Stockholm Syndrome? Did I need to see a professional about my attraction to the man that forced me to suck his cock in exchange for more dinner?

But it didn't stop there.

Raniero came back after dinner to find me on the windowsill again, picking up where I'd left off in the Tudor Era story. I was going to set the book to the side and indulge him in conversation, but he shook his head at me.

I let him maneuver my body how he wanted it. He placed the book on the windowsill seat, open to the page that I was on. Then he had me bend over, arms on either side of the book. "Read," he ordered as he pulled down my panties. "Aloud," he added after a moment.

I made it through a line before I felt the tip of his cock at my entrance. I clammed up immediately, looking over my shoulder to make eye contact with him.

Raniero's hand came down on my ass hard, leaving a stinging mark in its wake. I hissed from the pain but I had to admit, it made the feeling of his cock entering me so much better. "I said read aloud," he glared at me. "Do as you're told."

I turned back to the book and my eyes failed to focus on the words. I could stumble through three or four words before I had to take a deep breath and concentrate. The sensation of his cock sliding in and out of my pussy was distracting. Every time I took longer than a few seconds to get to the next sentence, Raniero spanked me. He brought his hand down on my pale skin and turned it cherry red.

I was lost to the pain and pleasure when I came all over his dick. The book was forgotten as I grabbed onto the pillows, the windowpane, the drapes, anything to keep myself upright as he made my thighs quiver from pleasure. He used that as an excuse to keep slapping my ass. Over and over again his cock rammed into my center and his hand came down on my ass. I threw my head back and rode out the sensations.

By morning the achiness that he'd predicted had set in. My thighs were sore and so was my ass—both from the spanking and the subsequent workout. But the part that really felt like it'd been bruised and beaten up was my pussy.

I wanted to take it easy, but having sex for the first time seemed to trigger something in Raniero. He turned into a depraved monster that wanted to be inside of me all the time.

I barely made it through breakfast before he was taking me to the gardens and fucking me under the morning sun. It didn't help the soreness at all and when he confiscated my panties, shoving them into his pants pocket before I could put them back on, I was forced to walk back to the house with his jizz dripping down my thighs.

"That's a good look on you," he said with a grin. "Wouldn't mind seeing it every day."

The sex felt good, but I was still afraid of getting knocked up. Any day now I could escape, have him arrested, and go back to living my life as though nothing happened. I could be myself again. But every time he came inside of me was one more chance that he could ruin my plans.

Not that I had any idea how I was going to escape. Sampson was everywhere all the time. I don't know how. For a big guy, he was surprisingly agile. On more than one occasion I caught him running around the property at sunrise or sunset and he looked like he was in good shape. If Sampson wasn't around, one of Raniero's other employees was. They all regarded me with the highest respect, but I saw them watching me out of the corner of their eyes. They were instructed to stop me if I tried to leave; I didn't need to hear it to know that it was true.

Raniero himself was in and out of the house at random. Sometimes I'd hear the garage door open in the dead of night. The first time I heard it, I asked him about it the next day. Raniero told me he had business to attend to. I couldn't help but notice that his left hand was wrapped in a bandage and he had a shiner. I hoped that whatever business he was attending to had gotten it worse than he had.

When Raniero was at home, he was either with me or in his office. He allowed Sampson to escort me on walks on days that he was too busy to do so himself. When I tried to worm what he was doing in there out of his bodyguard, Sampson shut down.

On the rare occasion that Raniero wasn't bogged down in work or missing from the mansion, he was fucking me. He'd come into my room and see me watching television. Then in a matter of moments, Netflix would keep playing the show while I was forced to ride on top of Raniero. Or he'd find me and Sampson in the library and he'd send his bodyguard away. With my book discarded, he'd press me up against the library's shelves as he held me aloft and jackhammered into me. The spines of some of Charles Dickens's greatest works were briefly tattooed on my skin.

Every time he fucked me, he ignored my pleas to come on my stomach or thigh. I think it turned him on to listen to me begging for him to come on my tits instead of inside me.

Raniero was hell-bent on getting me pregnant. And he was determined to make me want it. He'd wait until I orgasmed before shooting his load inside of me and refusing to pull out until a good twenty minutes had passed. He'd tease and torment me all the while, reminding me how much my body responded to him and how he knew I was turned on by his dirty talk. "You like it when I fill your pussy and tell you how I'm gonna do it again. It makes you crazy. You buck like a fucking bronco every time we go for round two."

And just like that, he'd be thrusting inside of me again. His cock would awaken whatever beast inside of me wanted to be fucked and stuffed so badly. It was delicious. It was horrifying. And I loved and hated every minute of it.

My life became a cycle. Wake, eat, fuck, sleep— not always in that order. My day was dictated by Raniero's schedule. And his schedule sometimes called for me to be in his bed.

Raniero's room was the opposite of mine. It had a view that overlooked the lake. While my room was decorated with light-colored blankets and white walls, his room had dimmed lighting and dark furniture. He told me that complete darkness helped him sleep better.

On the nights that he called me to his room, he warned me that the house was alarmed and Sampson's door was across the hall. "If he hears this door open, he's been instructed to stop you. If you fail to comply, he'll shoot you. Non-lethally, of course," Raniero added with a smile. "I wouldn't want the prize I worked so hard for to die."

And by hard he meant that he'd started taking pictures of us and sharing them on social media. "It's all part of the ruse, baby." He claimed that the police had stopped looking for my kidnapper when the photos came out. "People said you're notoriously hard to get ahold of anyway. I've had Sampson going to your place every few days and keeping up appearances. He stomps around, plays loud music, and I think he even brought a woman over once to fuck in your bed. But he had to," Raniero clucked his tongue, "we needed your neighbors to think you were having rowdy sex. Your landlord sent you a warning a few days ago, actually. If you don't keep it down, you might be evicted."

For some reason, that angered me. Even though my apartment wasn't the pinnacle of better living, it was still mine. Raniero could instruct Sampson to bring as much of my stuff as he wanted, but it didn't make me feel any better.

"Everyone thinks you're happy now, Calliope. So be happy." Then he'd strip off my clothes, lick my pussy, and use my screams against me. By the end of the night, I'd be full of his cum and ashamed of myself for being turned on by this crazy, monster of a man.

He was a sweet man sometimes, but like Jekyll and Hyde, he'd flip a switch and become a tyrant. I couldn't figure out if I was falling in love with him or plotting his death. Raniero Valenti was steadily ruining my life and all I could do about it was spread my legs and let him fuck me one more time.

One day I'd wake up and know what to do next. I just didn't know when that day would come.

13

RANIERO

Four weeks and three days. That's all it took for me to get here.

Calliope is curled up beside me, her ass pressed against my raging boner. I try to remain still so as to not wake her. She is breathtaking bathed in the soft morning light.

My brothers were right; I needed to fuck Calliope to break her. Sometimes I see a subversive look in her eyes when she sees an open door or thinks she might be able to escape, but she never runs. I know that she isn't wholly mine yet, but we're getting there.

Last night I told her that I loved her. Cock buried in her soaked pussy, I pressed my forehead to hers and whispered the words. She pretended not to hear, but I know she did.

I think I'll make her breakfast this morning. A chorizo omelet with chipotle adobo salsa. A bowl of freshly picked and washed berries with a drizzle of sugar to bring out the juices. I'll even hand-squeeze a glass of orange juice for her.

I hate to extract myself from the bed like this, but I think she'll be much happier when I return with a homemade plate of food. I slip on a pair of boxers and head to the kitchen.

Grace is startled. She's in the middle of her morning routine when I enter the kitchen whistling. She jumps a foot in the air and comes down with her fists up. She's ready to throw punches.

"Calm down, Grace," I hold up my hands apologetically. "It's just me."

"Mr. Valenti," she breathes. Her hands come up to her chest as if she's trying to soothe her racing heart. "You scared me!"

She chastises me like my mother used to and it brings a smile to my lips. Though I talk to my parents every Sunday night, I can't deny that I miss them. I visit Italy twice a year—once in the summer and once during the holidays. They visit the states twice a year, usually a couple of months after my visits. The family gets together for a big Valenti family dinner and mother pries into our personal lives. She wants to know how we're seeing, how serious it is, and if we'll be getting married soon. Up until now, the five of us have always beat around the marriage bush, but I'll have something to share at our next family reunion.

"I just want to make breakfast for Calliope. I didn't mean to scare you, Grace." But she's already shaking her head and mumbling under her breath. She's always a little standoffish when something unexpected happens.

I busy myself with cracking eggs and cooking meat. As everything cooks, I grab some berries from the fridge and toss them into a bowl. It's all going as planned until Calliope appears in the kitchen door frame wearing one of my shirts as a dress. "Sorry to interrupt," she raises her voice after a few moments, "I just wasn't sure where you'd gone."

Grace whispers a few words in Italian under her breath that sound suspiciously like *good heavens, they're sleeping together.* Then she pulls on a smile before announcing that she needs to go pick some herbs from the garden.

It's odd to see her race away from an uncomfortable scene, but Grace doesn't like to get involved in matters that don't affect her. She'd rather bury herself in work than have to listen to me and the others engage in business talk. The less she knows, the better off she'll be if the police ever come knocking.

"I'm making you breakfast," I gesture toward the bowl of fruit. "I thought it would be nice if you woke up and had a hot meal." My mother used to bring us breakfast in bed on our birthdays. I remember waking up at five in the morning, a year older than I was the day before, and waiting as patiently as I could for my mom to bring my favorite meal. There are some traditions of my youth that I want to continue.

Calliope takes a few tentative steps into the kitchen. "Thank you," she says with a half-hearted smile. "That's very nice of you."

I want to tell her that she hasn't seen anything yet. When everything settles down and she doesn't look like she's going to run the first chance she gets, she'll see a whole new side of me. "Take a seat. I'm just finishing up the omelet now."

There's a small dining table in front of the window that seats no more than four. I used to use it most mornings when I didn't have time for a format breakfast, but ever since Calliope arrived, we've been using the formal dining room. She grabs a seat and runs her hands over the tops of her thighs to smooth out the fabric of the shirt.

"I think you scandalized Grace," I joke as I start delivering Calliope's meal in parts. First, her fruit, then, the orange juice. She uses her fingers to pop a strawberry into her mouth as I return to the stove to check on the omelet.

"I wasn't sure what else to wear," she says with a blush. "I woke up and you weren't there. I wasn't sure if I was supposed to go back to my room or what. I probably should have waited for you to return." Calliope turns toward the window so I can't see her face anymore. "I'm sorry I didn't stay in your room."

It doesn't matter to me what she does, so long as she does what I want her to. And I want her to spend time with me, fall in love with me, and live happily ever after with me. That doesn't mean I have to control her every action. "This is going to be your home, Calliope. You are free to roam around as you please." With only one unspoken rule: *don't run away.*

I plate her omelet and sprinkle some freshly grated cheese on top. I'll have to thank Grace for all the work that she does. "I hope you're hungry this morning," I announce with a cheerful smile as I drop the plate in front of her. "It's a chorizo omelet. Let me grab the salsa!"

I didn't make the chipotle adobo salsa from scratch. I know my way around a kitchen, but I was relying on Grace having some in the fridge. It's my favorite salsa for breakfast food, tacos, and chips. I pull out the container and start scooping some into a bowl when I catch Calliope out of the corner of my eye.

Her nose is crinkled in disgust as she brings her fork to the omelet and starts to dissect it. Steam wafts from the meat, cheese, and eggs so I know it's not underdone. Just as I'm about to ask her what's wrong, she gets up from the table and bolts.

The fork clatters to the ground. "What the hell!" I glare at Calliope's fast-moving figure. She only makes it to the kitchen sink before she starts vomiting.

My first thought is that Grace is going to be pissed that she has to clean this up. I set down the container of salsa and walk over to Calliope and gather her hair in my hands. With one hand acting as a ponytail, the other rubs her back gently. I can clean this up. Grace does too much for this household to be responsible for cleaning up Calliope's messes.

Calliope smacks my hand away after a few seconds. "You're an asshole," she groans as she spins in place and sinks to the floor. Her face has turned as white as a sheet and she buries it in her hands.

"Me?" I glare down at her. "What did I do?"

She lifts her head long enough to give me a pointed look as if asking if I'm serious. When I don't respond, she scoffs and slams her head back down between her legs. "This is all your fault," comes her muffled accusation.

I'm about to tell her that she better start to explain before I get angry when it dawns on me. "Calliope," I grab onto the kitchen sink to steady myself, "are you pregnant?" I try to do the math but it doesn't make sense to me. I should have tracked Calliope's cycle. She hasn't had a period in the four weeks that she's been here, but she likely had it before I kidnapped her.

She groans and whimpers, an inadequate response to my question. "When was your last period?" I should have asked that ages ago. The day I started fucking her, for example. But I didn't expect to deflower her so quickly.

"I don't know," she mumbles. "A week before I

was brought here? A week and a half?" Calliope lets out a whimper that's half tears. "You're psychotic, you know that?"

Now the math is starting to add up. Pregnancy dating starts on the first day of your last menstrual cycle. If I conservatively say that it was a week before I kidnapped her, then that would make her five weeks along. Give or take a few days. "You need to take a pregnancy test."

Calliope glares up at me. "Vomiting isn't enough of an indicator?"

It's a start, but it isn't a positive pee stick. I leave the room and take the stairs two and a time. When I first started fucking Calliope into submission, I ordered pregnancy tests online in bulk. A pack of ten showed up at the door a week later and I kept them stashed in a hallway closet where I was sure no one would come across them.

I grab the oversized box and rip it open, pulling out the first plastic-wrapped test that I can get my hands on. The instructions are probably the same as all the rest: pee on the stick, wait until a result pops up. So I don't waste any time reading literature on how to make sure you get the best possible sample.

I'm ripping the damn plastic off the pregnancy test before I even make it all the way back to

Calliope. It's a standard little stick with a cap on the end and I shove it at her as I walk up. "Take this. Now."

She stares at the pregnancy test and then reluctantly takes in from my hand. When I offer to help her to her feet, she doesn't accept. "You're a fucking sicko."

God, I want to slam my cock between her lips and make her taste punishment on her tongue. But I point toward the hallway where the bathroom is and tell her to move it instead. "We'll discuss your bad behavior later." I pretend not to see her rolling her eyes at me.

Calliope mumbles incoherently under her breath but I catch a word here and there. The word is always *jackass*.

Frankly, I don't care what she calls me, just as long as she's pregnant. Once I get a baby on her, the plan can move forward. I've already been planning the wedding in my limited spare time, but it'll be nice to get Calliope a ring, get down on one knee, and promise that the rest of her life will be better with me by her side.

When we reach the hall bathroom, Calliope walks in and goes to shut the door behind her, but I stop it with a flat palm. "You're kidding me," she looks up at me in disgust. "You're going to watch me pee?"

It isn't my kink, but I want to see what that pregnancy test says. "I'll stare at the wall," I decide after a moment. "But I want you to leave the door open." I control her life. She does what I say.

Calliope's mutterings become even more angered as she walks inside and waits for me to turn around. I take a step to the side and lean up against the wall with my arms crossed impatiently over my chest. I hear the slam of plastic on the counter and it's followed a few seconds later by the sound of her peeing. This is definitely not my kink.

A few moments later, as I'm trying to decide which room in the house will be the new nursery, I hear the toilet flush. "I'm decent," Calliope growls just a second before the sink comes on.

I come around the door frame and let myself in. The pregnancy test is sitting on the counter with the purple cap placed back on the end she peed on.

"I've never taken one of those before," she says with an accusatory glare. "I just had to assume that was the side I peed on since you didn't give me any instructions."

She *was* a virgin when I kidnapped her off the streets. There's no reason to shell out $7 a test when you know for sure you aren't pregnant. "I'm sorry," I apologize with a purse of my lips. "I guess I didn't know that."

Calliope dries her hands on the towel hanging in front of the shower. There's silence in the room for a minute before she says, "There's a lot about me that you don't know, Raniero. Your file can tell you my sealed criminal history and my medical records, but it won't tell you who I am."

Maybe so, but we have the rest of our lives to get to know one another. I hold up the pregnancy test with two clear pink lines in the test window. "You can tell me who you are over dinner for the next forty years."

Her face falls when sees the test window. I think I even feel the frustration when her hand comes up to rest on her belly. "I-I think I need to lie down."

I'm not a fool. I know that she feels out of her depth. This isn't a situation any woman could be brought into and expected to handle with grace and dignity. I take a few steps toward her and press my lips to her forehead. "Take all the time you need. Let me know if you need anything."

I don't bother following her up the stairs or locking her bedroom door. I just give her some space while I sit on the bathroom floor and stare at the two pink lines.

It wasn't until I was twenty-four years old that I really started thinking about having a family and settling down. But as the years passed, I seemed to get further and further from that dream. My father told me that family comes first; he didn't mean the Valentis as a whole. He meant finding a woman to love and having children. He always said that having a family was the greatest thing that ever happened to him.

I know Calliope doesn't see it now, but one day she'll realize that I did her a favor. All this was for the two of us. It was meant to be.

Some might even call it fate.

14

CALLIOPE

Once upon a time, I wanted to be a teacher. It's a foolish dream that every kid has when they come across a teacher that changes their life. But a lot of them grow up and go into other careers. They become mechanics, they run convenience stores or restaurants, they go into law or politics, or some other job that pays better than a teacher's salary. Hell, even I waited tables and went into real estate instead of following my dreams.

But if I'd become a teacher, maybe I wouldn't be locked up in an ivory tower belonging to a rich Villain Charming.

I can't seem to make myself comfortable when I come back to my room. The bed feels too cushy, the taste of wealth making me nauseous again. When I switch to the windowsill, I feel restless looking out at the beautiful garden below when everything feels dark and heavy. The sitting area feels too stuffy and I don't want to take a bath.

I settle for lying on the floor with my extremities splayed out in an X. The white ceiling is my only comfort.

Raniero's house is everything I dreamt of as a kid. Bright white walls with picture frames acting as the only pop of color. Plenty of space for the family to stretch out in without ever feeling like they were crowding one another. Everything draped in comfort and blankets, beckoning friends and visitors to sit down and stay a while.

I thought that I'd wind up in a house like this because I'd married a man that I loved. I didn't have a clear picture of what he looked like, but I knew that he worked hard. One of those guys that takes his forty hours a week seriously. When he came home at night, he'd leave the office at the front door. He wouldn't sully our home with talk about corporate regulations and work stresses because he'd rather spend time with me and the children.

Children. Just thinking about kids makes me bring a hand up to my stomach.

I've been thin for as long as I could remember.

First, it was because I was young and my metabolism burned off the calories within an hour. Then, it was because I couldn't afford to eat. I physically cannot imagine what my body will look like swollen with a baby.

I know that a lot of women dream about being mothers when they're twenty-five. I should feel lucky that it happened to me so quickly and with someone who can provide for me. But I just feel empty inside. I can't process everything that's happened.

My thoughts race the Daytona 500 around my head, ping-ponging off the walls of my brain as they crash into one another. What will my wedding be like? What will I tell my children about their father? Will I ever be allowed to leave this house again? Will Raniero allow me to have a career? What do I even want to do?

There are so many questions and the only answers that I can find are half-baked conclusions that don't make any sense.

I take a deep breath and try to center myself. *Breathe in peace, breathe out anger.* I scream those words in my head over the thousands of questions I don't have answers for. Eventually, the yells drown out the questions and all I'm left with is a little voice in my head telling me to breathe in peace and breathe out anger.

The room feels like it's spinning so I shut my eyes. "This wasn't how it was supposed to go," I whisper to no one in particular. The room is empty; I'm not talking to anyone except myself.

I was supposed to have a mom and a dad that loved one another. They were supposed to be together forever. My dad wasn't supposed to hit my mom or scream at her for whatever perceived fault he could dream up. She wasn't supposed to run away and leave me and my brothers to fend for ourselves.

Ares and Apollo were older than me and they protected me the best they could. But Ares was into sports and Apollo was in every club that would take him. When they were busy with practices and after-school meetings, I was listening to my father rant about how I looked like my mother and that I was just as worthless. Then while I was praying for my brothers to walk through the door and bust up the scene, my father would hit me. He said that it was repayment for my mother's sins, that a woman is only as strong as the man she has in her life. "Your mother has no one and she is weak. You have me and you will be strong." He drilled those words into me with a fist to the gut. "Pain only makes you stronger, sweetie. Remember that."

Life wasn't supposed to turn out that way. I was supposed to make it through high school with straight A's taking honor classes and advanced placement English. The college credits that I earned from those classes would put me ahead when I finally started college. I was going to get my teaching degree and change lives.

I was going to do good things.

I went to a church once when I was sixteen. I had just finished up my junior year and a teacher sent a report home stating that I kept coming into class late. I know she thought that she was being helpful, but my dad didn't see it that way. He fractured my wrist and stabilized it with a first aid wrap he found under the bathroom sink. He told me I needed to do better if I was going to make him proud, then he left for work.

I stumbled from the house with all the bones in my body aching. He'd pushed me into walls and shoved me to the floor. I felt battered and broken and I went to the only place that I could think of that treated battered and broken people without asking any questions.

The doors of the Methodist church were

unlocked and there were arrows pointing me toward the pastor's office. Instead, I took a seat in the back row of the pews and stared at the cross on the stage. There were no bibles for me to flip through, just a few different hymnals on the back of the pew in front of me. I skipped through the pages searching for answers, only finding music that worshipped Him.

"Miss, can I help you?" Someone asked after a while.

I don't know when I started crying, but I guess somewhere between hymn 518 from one book and 1,024 in another, my eyes started leaking. "Why do bad things happen to good people?" I asked the guy standing at the end of the pew.

He gave me a shrug before climbing inside and taking a seat on the other end. "He has a plan for everything. He takes your pain and uses it to make you stronger."

I'm sure the man meant well, but his words sounded just like my father's and they made my stomach churn with anger and frustration. I fled from the church with no more answers than I'd walked through the door with.

I never went to college like I thought I would. I ran away from home instead. I could have applied for loans or gone to the battered woman's shelter, but I slept on park benches and tried to fend for myself.

I always dreamt of something better. I always said that one day my time would come. I just didn't think it would come with so many strings.

Raniero could have been a game-changer if the circumstances were different. If he loved me... if we'd dated... if he treated me with respect... all the if's. If he wasn't himself, all of this might be okay.

But everyone knows about the Valenti family. We've all heard the rumors about Mateo Valenti going to prison for murder. We've joked about Luca holding a place on the City Council. We've made fun of Stefano and Cesare for following in the family's footsteps. Everybody knows that the Valentis came by their fortune through illegal means. We all just sort of thought they were a joke. Dangerous, but a joke.

I never expected to be kidnapped by Raniero. I didn't even think about what I'd do if he kept me locked up in his home. How was I supposed to prepare for his charm, sex appeal, and twisted lust? Nobody ever tells you what to do when you find yourself backed into a corner with a feral dog that just wants to make you feel good. There isn't a guidebook on how to control yourself when your hormones are demanding that you get off just one more time.

It wasn't supposed to be like this. My life was supposed to be a fairytale, not a horror movie.

15

RANIERO

"I figure if we have the wedding before the end of your first trimester, you won't be showing. You'll still look slim and beautiful in the photos and people won't think it's a shotgun wedding." Except for Grant Jackson, who will personally be getting an invitation from me that says *now that I've knocked your daughter up, I guess I better marry her.* Calliope doesn't need to worry about that though. "That leaves us about seven weeks, but I'm thinking if we get married in four, people can even speculate that we got pregnant on our wedding night."

Calliope stares at the coffee mug in front of her and shrugs her shoulders. "Yeah, sure," she mumbles, the words slurring together as if she's drunk.

I turn my back to her and tighten my jaw in frustration. It's been a week since we learned of her pregnancy and she's been moping ever since. I catch her lying on the floor of her bedroom or sitting outside in the garden, always with the same dull, far-off expression on her face. I know that this was never what she predicted for her life, but she can't be this upset over how it turned out.

I've tried keeping my mouth shut, but I'm growing weary of the depression she's settled into. It's like being pregnant turned off all the lights in her house and she's been shuttered away in the darkness. "My cousin would like to come by this weekend and take you dress shopping. How does that sound?"

She doesn't look up from her mug. "Sounds good."

I close my eyes and count to ten as I try to keep my anger under control. I know that this isn't ideal. I *know* that I fucked up by not earning her trust first. But what can I do to say that I'm sorry? How can I make her see that it won't always be like this? "Is something wrong, Calliope?" I turn around slowly and push my back into the countertop, relishing the pain as it distracts me from my fury.

Calliope's head shakes a couple of times and then she reaches up to wipe her face. As she gets up from her seat, she avoids looking at me. "I have to use the bathroom," she mumbles as she skirts out of the kitchen. But she doesn't head down the hall, she just runs upstairs.

Thank God she's gone because I throw the first thing I can grab at the wall. A plate shatters in a spectacular display of ceramic fireworks. "What the fuck is her problem?" I growl.

Grace had the good sense to disappear when we came into the kitchen a little bit ago, but she returns when she hears the plate shatter. "Oh, dear," she frowns as she grabs a broom, "is something wrong, Mr. Valenti?"

I don't confide in Grace because she has a job and she does it well. She's in charge of the kitchen, whether it be cooking meals, stocking, or cleaning up. She isn't my personal therapist and she doesn't deserve to be treated like one. I snap my teeth together to keep from spilling all my frustrations on her.

She hums to herself as she sweeps up my mess. As

Grace waits for a response, I see her casually flicking her gaze in my direction. But when I am not forthcoming, she takes it upon herself to give me some advice. "You treat me like family, Mr. Valenti, and I appreciate that. I know that I will never have to worry again as long as you're around. But not everybody knows that."

Grace doesn't say much, but she says what's important. I stand there and watch as she finishes cleaning up the ceramic mess. With each breath, I calm myself down. I need to talk to Calliope like she's an equal. I've viewed her as my prisoner since the day I kidnapped her and that's probably how she's viewing herself. She needs to know that she means more to me than that.

Before leaving the kitchen, I walk over to Grace and give her a hug. "Thanks," I whisper in her ear, "I appreciate having you in my family."

It feels like a long climb up the stairs to the second floor. Each step weighs on my soul like an anvil. I'm not sure how to change the dynamic that I've created between Calliope and me, but I know that it has to change if we're ever going to get past this.

I dread standing in front of her door. There's a sense of impending doom throbbing in my chest. It takes everything in me to knock on the door instead of opening it and letting myself in.

As per usual, I find her lying on the floor with her eyes trained on the ceiling. "Calliope," I call her name like it's a question but she doesn't turn to look at me. "I think we should talk."

She sighs but otherwise doesn't move. "If it's about the wedding, we can do whatever you want. I don't care."

That one hurts and I don't know why. I awkwardly walk over and take a seat on the floor beside her. I don't know when I last sat criss-cross apple sauce, but it's the first thing that I think of when I make myself comfortable. "I need you to talk to me, Calliope. I need you to tell me what's wrong. I know this situation isn't ideal, but it's what we have and I want to make you feel better."

Calliope turns her head to the side to look at me. Her eyes look dead. "This situation isn't *ideal*?" She repeats my words back to me. "You think I wanted to be kidnapped, held hostage, knocked up, and married to a man I barely know?"

"That's not what I meant," I try to backpedal but she doesn't let me.

"You think this is what I pictured for my life? Marrying someone out of revenge to get back at my father? You don't put your hands on me like he did, but you're no better than him. He hurt me out of spite for my mother and you hurt me out of spite for him." She huffs and turns back to face the ceiling. "I'm tired of being the one to pay my parents' debts."

She makes me feel like the world's biggest asshole, with good reason, too. I might have gathered a file full of information on her, but it didn't really tell me the important things. "Calliope, let's take your father out of the equation for a moment. If it wasn't for him, I never would have found you."

"You never would have wanted to," she adds with a minute shrug of her shoulders.

"That's not true," I frown. "I would have wanted to find out, I just didn't know that it was *you* I was looking for." I struggle to put together the right words for what I'm feeling. Everything sounds too mushy and romantic and I'm not that guy. "I didn't know who you were until your father entered the picture. I wanted to hurt him as badly as he hurt me and that's how I found you. And I know it's wrong to keep you here, but I don't want to let you go."

I reach out to draw my fingers along her forearm. I love touching Calliope because she's so soft and warm. Touching her feels like coming home after a long day and climbing into bed. It's comforting. "You're a beautiful young woman, Calliope. You persevere despite all that life has thrown at you. You're the bravest person I've ever met. I don't any other woman that would be escorted through the front doors with a gun pointed at her back and not freak out. You've adapted to everything I've thrown at you and managed to come out stronger on the other side. And I know it must be tiring being so strong, which is why you don't have to be anymore."

Slowly she turns her head again. Her gaze is questioning despite the deep V of her eyebrows. "What do you mean?"

I curl my fingers around her wrist and bring it toward me. As I stare at her barren ring finger, I know what I have to do. "You've spent your entire life fighting to stay afloat. You have been the strong, confident woman that everyone expected you to be even when life threatened to pull you under. But not anymore. I'm going to take care of you, Calliope. I'm going to be your strength from now on."

I should have said these words from the start, but I wouldn't have meant them. Hell, I'm surprised that I mean them now. I've loved Calliope the way a predator loves their prey, but knowing that my child is growing inside of her changes my feelings completely. "Your father will never touch you again. You'll never have to see him again if you don't want to. If what I'm forcing you into having isn't what you want, I'll let you go and I'll make sure you're never homeless again. You're carrying my baby, Calliope, and that changes the shift of power in this relationship. You hold all the cards now. Tell me what you want and I'll make it happen."

Calliope just stares at me. The seconds turn into minutes and the stretch of silence between us fills the room. I'm starting to wonder if she's going to make me release her when she says that she wants to work with children.

"What?" I frown.

She is silent again, this time even longer. But I realize it's because she's gathering her thoughts. "I don't want to be a housewife or a stay-at-home mom. I want to work with kids, maybe in a preschool or something. Part-time," Calliope adds, "because I want to get my teaching degree. Or maybe do something in school counseling. I needed someone who understood what I was going through back in junior high and high school. I think I could be that someone for other kids."

I'm blown away. I expected her to tell me to release her post-haste. I expected to write her a check for an inconceivable sum just so that she'd let me see my child again one day. I expected her to run from me as quickly as possible. "You want to go to school?"

Calliope nods her head yes. "I want to be the hero I never had until I met you."

I don't even know what to say. I open my mouth to speak and then close it real quick, unable to summon the right words.

"What you did was wrong, Raniero, but I think you're more than capable of spending the rest of your life making up for it." A hint of a smile appears on her lips and it breathes new life into me.

"I can't change the past, but I promise you that the future will be everything you ever hoped it would be." She has made dreams come true that I didn't even know I had.

I don't know what Calliope's happily ever after looks like just yet, but when I find out, I'll do everything in my power to make it happen.

Maybe I should send Grant Jackson a fruit basket. If it wasn't for his vendetta against the Valenti family, I wouldn't have found his daughter.

CALLIOPE

*T*ime is relative. The rate at which it passes depends on your frame of reference.

The minutes pass in nausea. The doctor says it generally abates around the end of the first trimester, but for now, I walk around with a sleeve of crackers and suck on popsicles. Someone on a mom forum said the sugar helps combat feeling sick, so now I live off of orange popsicles and saltines.

The days pass in prenatal vitamins. They're the size of horse pills and I gag when I swallow them. "Come on," Raniero jokes, "I've seen you swallow bigger loads than that." My cheeks turn bright pink in reference to our first night together. After a few days, I start cutting them in half. A horse pill is easier to swallow when it isn't whole.

The weeks pass in food comparisons. At five weeks pregnant, my baby is the size of an apple seed. At six weeks, a sweet pea. At seven weeks, a blueberry. At eight weeks, a raspberry. Every time Raniero tells me a different food item, I bury my face in a pillow and weep. I'm not sad about being pregnant anymore, I'm sad I can't eat.

Everything else just happens to me, like the story of my life that I'm being told for the first time.

Raniero immediately set me up with an obstetrician. We sat in a sterile medical office with the smell of lavender evading our nostrils and tried to pretend that we were normal people, me more so than him. He'd offered to bring someone directly to the house, but I jumped at the chance to get out of the mansion. My first taste of Manhattan in all its glory felt like returning home.

No buildings had been erected in my absence. Construction of the most traveled upon roads continued. Nothing major had happened in the four weeks I'd been locked up like a caged animal. But somehow the trees seemed fuller and the streets seemed busier. It made me feel alive.

But when we reached the Women's Health

Group and a nurse walked me back to my room with a handful of questions, I felt uneasy. I couldn't remember the exact date of my last menstrual period because the app that tracked that sort of thing was on my phone, which I didn't have. I couldn't explain to the doctor that although we were trying to have a baby, I was not married to Raniero nor had we been together for long. He took the reins on that one and defended my discomfort with half-truths. "Her father is the police chief and he doesn't really like me, so it's been a very tenuous courtship, at best."

My father was the police chief. He didn't like Raniero. Our courtship had been tenuous. But he failed to mention that it was because he kidnapped me from an open house and kept me locked in his mansion acting as his personal sex slave.

"Oh, so you're the girl they thought went missing," the doctor said with a sort of half smile. "Until that second week when you started posting pictures on social media, everybody was really concerned."

I tried to laugh it off, but it was something I was going to have to deal with for weeks. People would question my sudden return to Manhattan. They'd ask why I left my open house without even locking the door behind me. And why did I leave my stuff on the counter? There would be a hundred questions I'd have to answer and all I could do was shrink into myself and hope that Raniero had a plan.

The doctor ordered a pregnancy test to confirm that I was, indeed, pregnant, and then she put me on prenatal vitamins. Raniero asked about various dietary supplements. Could I take iron pills during my pregnancy? What about vitamin C? Probiotics? Potassium? He had a list in his head and raffled off the items one after the other.

He also asked about an exercise regimen. "It isn't that I don't want her to get big. I understand that she's growing a child in there. But I'm an avid runner and I know that some exercise during pregnancy can help prevent gestational diabetes."

The doctor nodded her head in agreement. "As long as the mother doesn't currently have diabetes," she added, "then it can help reduce the risk. I'd say if mom is feeling up to it," she looked at me with a smile, "she can continue any exercises she's currently doing and work up to any others she wants to do as long as there isn't any pain."

With all of our questions answered, we were halfway out of the door when the doctor stopped us. "Also, and I hate saying this part, I always suggest that my patients keep the exciting news to themselves until twelve or thirteen weeks. That's the end of the first trimester and when your risk for miscarriage drops dramatically. I'm not saying you can't tell your family and friends," she said gently, "I'm just informing you of the risks. It's a lot harder to tell people that you miscarried than it is to tell them that you're pregnant."

I grabbed my belly in fear and felt Raniero's hand reach out to hold my elbow. "Thank you for letting us know, doctor. We'll keep that in mind."

I could barely get to the car on my own. Raniero had to help me with an arm around my waist while he supported most of my weight. "What if I miscarry?" I hadn't even realized that I cared that much. "What if I do something that hurts the baby?" I thought I was just going along with Raniero's plan, but now all I could think about was sitting still and willing this child in my womb to grow strong and healthy.

Raniero crouched outside of my door and brought my hand to his lips. He placed a flurry of kisses on my palm before bringing it up to rest on his cheek. "You're going to be fine, Calliope. I'm going to take care of you. We'll go pick up the prenatals the doctor ordered and then we'll figure out if there's anything we can do to keep you safe. The best foods to eat, the best exercises to do, the best everything. We'll figure it out, Calli, together. You, me, and baby against the world."

His words calmed my fears. In the weeks that came after, he followed through with all his promises.

He plied me with questions about the wedding night and day, but when he felt like my energy was waning, he'd take on the decisions for himself. I dreamt about my wedding and I wanted a fairytale affair like everybody else, but some days it was just too much.

When Raniero wanted me to add my friends to the guest list, I didn't even know what to say. Sure, I had friends sprinkled throughout the city, but many of them had stopped being so kind after I spent a few weeks on their couches. Others, well, I wasn't sure how close those friendships were considering we hadn't spoken since high school.

But once again, Raniero took everything upon himself. The only real decision I had to make was what I wanted to wear.

"You can wear a paper bag if you'd like," Raniero offered over breakfast one morning. He'd told Grace that I was pregnant and she was delighted. She started rattling off different foods I couldn't eat and what she would substitute them with. I think she was more excited than Raniero and I put together.

Grace was the one that said I couldn't wear *whatever* I wanted. She was in the room when Raniero said I could wear a paper bag and she almost dropped the tray of pancakes. "No, honey," she looked at me, "this is your big day. No paper bags. You're going to be the belle of the ball. If anything, you need a gown like Cinderella's."

She was the only person that I allowed to push me around. With Raniero's approval, she took me to a little boutique in a small town forty miles away. "My friend makes beautiful wedding gowns. You tell her what you want and she'll make it happen." We spent the afternoon drunk on laughter and friendship. For the first time in years, I had a girls' day and I loved it.

Everything changed overnight, it felt like. Raniero didn't lock my bedroom door anymore and he trusted me to stroll the grounds without an escort. Sampson was always around, but he didn't look at me like a flight risk anymore. He regarded me as Raniero's equal, always endeavoring to do the littlest thing if it made my life easier.

He was the one that drove me to various

daycares in the area. The first day he pulled up in front of one, he said that he was working on Raniero's wishes. "He said that you want to work with children. My mother has run this place since I was a kid." Sampson sheepishly blushed. "We thought it'd be a great place for you to get some hands-on experience."

My life sort of settled into a routine. Mornings with Grace and Raniero where we talked about how I was feeling and what I was craving. Raniero would have flown to Italy and gotten me a bowl of the freshest pasta if that's what I asked for. Grace was willing to whip up anything, including a remedy for my morning sickness. She gave me a steaming cup of tea every morning that she said would cure my nausea for the day. Maybe it did or maybe it was a placebo. Regardless, she saved me from vomiting every hour for the next few weeks.

In the afternoons, I spent time at one daycare or another. I learned to change diapers, make formula, properly thaw and heat breastmilk, and more. I took care of children as young as six weeks old and as old as five. I experienced a lifetime of memories in those four weeks.

My evenings were spent with Raniero. Sometimes he made me dinner, but more often than not, an evening cook came by to finish whatever Grace had prepared in the morning. We ate in the kitchen nook, the formal dining room, and sometimes curled up together on the couch. Raniero allowed me to go wherever I wanted. "You're carrying my child," he'd whisper in my ear, "you can have the world."

Truly, he was a changed man. He still took me to bed religiously, praising the fullness of my breasts and the swell of my stomach. I couldn't see any change, but he swore every day that he noticed I was growing larger with his child. We'd make love, but sometimes we'd fuck. The difference was the words he whispered in my ear when he came inside of me. But not once did I shy away from him. I tried to say it was the hormones that made me want him, but Raniero knew better. I was falling for him with each passing day.

Our love story didn't start out conventionally, but it was going to have a happily ever after one day.

17

RANIERO

I'm fucking *nervous*. What kind of peasant bullshit is this?

"Take a shot," Mateo raises a shot glass in the air as if he can hear my thoughts. "I guarantee your face won't be sheet white when you walk down the aisle."

I turn around to pin him with a glare. "I should have asked Luca to be my best man."

From the couch, Luca nods his head in agreement and says, "Damn right, you should have. I'd have thrown a better bachelor party. For starters, we'd have been in Monaco and there would have been strippers."

My two younger brothers exchange glances. I haven't seen Stefano or Cesare in a couple of months. They say it's because I was too caught up in finding a wife and knocking her up, but I think they were too busy to drop by or schedule a lunch. "Could have found *me* a wife in Monaco," Cesare waggles his eyebrows.

I snort in response and head toward the mini-bar. "Don't you have a girl?"

Cesare rolls his eyes and starts to examine his cuticles. I swear he has his fingernails buffed once a week. "Worry about yourself, Nero, don't worry about me."

Every member of the Valenti family has something going on whether they want to admit it or not. Mateo has been chasing the woman he was engaged to before he was thrown in prison. Luca is blackmailing or being blackmailed by someone, I can't remember which. Stefano always has half a dozen women swarming around him like bees to a flower. And Cesare was hailed in the newspaper for saving a woman's life at the grocery store, a woman that looks suspiciously like the one whose pictures hang in his office.

The Valenti boys are dangerous and they always have something up their sleeve. I'll never understand how we got here. We used to just be five little kids racing around the idyllic gardens of our parents' estate, playing tag and hiding behind statues. Now we're queuing up to get married and start a family.

There's a knock on the hotel room door just a few seconds before it starts to open. My father walks in with a teary-eyed smile and starts telling me how proud he is of me in Italian. It's been a while since I've used the language and my understanding is rough, but I know what he means when he wraps his arms around me and pats me on the back.

"Do you have it?" I ask when he stops going on and on about how lovely everything looks.

Dad pats his breast pocket and then both his sides. It takes him only a second to pull out the little black box. "I had to get your mother an even bigger ring to replace this one, but she was so happy to hear that you were getting married."

I take the box from him and open it. Inside is the Valenti family engagement ring that has been in our family for over a century. It's been passed down from generation to generation, only to wind up in my hands. My brothers will never get the family ring, but I'm happy to pay for them to start their own. In a hundred years' time, there could be a dozen or more Valenti family rings running around, gracing the fingers of the women we love. But this one is mine and it is beautiful.

"She's going to love it, son," father says as he claps a hand on my shoulder. "She'll love it just because she loves you."

I worry about that some days. Calliope has only been with me for two months. Half the reason she's here is because of the requested guest of honor: her father. I wanted revenge so badly that I was willing to sign the rest of my life away to the police chief's daughter to get it. But the other half of the reason Calliope is here is because somewhere in between revenge and retribution, I found a woman that I wanted to be with. It was less about signing the rest of my life away and more about being with someone I truly loved.

"I love her." The words slip out of my mouth and form a crease on my forehead.

"No shit, buddy," Stefano says with a roll of his eyes. "Or else you wouldn't be marrying her." He doesn't know about everything, not yet, anyway. I haven't seen him long enough to tell him the saga. But in a way, he's right.

If I hadn't liked Calliope, keeping her trapped in my mansion would have been different. I might not have shoved my cock down her throat that first night. I might not have impregnated her with my child. I might have been more willing to blackmail Chief Jackson instead of embarrass him. Calliope is a beautiful, submissive, different sort of girl. I've never known anyone like her before. But if she'd have been someone else? Who knows if I'd have followed through with my threats?

A man can only allow himself to go so far for duty. I don't think I'd have married Calliope if she wasn't what I was searching for.

"I have to do something," I mumble after a second. I snap the box closed and head for the door.

"Wait," father calls after me, "where are you going?"

But I don't have time to slow down and tell him. I need to see Calliope. I need to talk to her before she walks down that aisle. She's on a floor above me and I race up the stairs instead of waiting for the elevator. I can hear laughter and music coming from her room as I approach.

Fist poised to knock, the door opens before I get a chance and I see my mother standing there with a laugh primed on her lips. She has an ice bucket in her hands and when she sees me, she almost drops it. "Nero," she says my name like a swear word, "what are you doing out here?"

"I need to see Calliope." I can't stress how much I need to see her. How I need to talk to her almost as much as I need to take my next breath.

Mother chastises me and pulls the door behind her until I can't fully see inside the room anymore. "It's bad luck to see the bride before the wedding. Go back to your room. You'll see her later," she urges

I press my hand to the hotel room door to stop my mom from shutting it completely. "Please," I beg, "I need to talk to her."

She sighs heavily and backs into the room, leaving the door cracked as she finds my bride. I hear her telling Calliope that I'm outside and want to talk, but that she doesn't have to see me before the wedding if she doesn't want to. I almost bang my head on the door frame at my mother's insistence on sticking to tradition.

"No, no," Calliope insists, "I'll see him."

My heart soars in response and I burst through the door before anyone can stop me. "I need to talk to you," are the first words out of my mouth and the whole room gasps in response. "Just a couple of minutes. Alone, if it's okay."

My mother glares at me. "You better not be backing out of this wedding, Nero. I didn't raise you like this!" She rewards me with a waggling finger that says I better not embarrass her.

"It's not that, mother. I just need to tell Calliope something before we go to the church." After ensuring that I don't plan to walk out on my pregnant wife, everyone filters out of the room slowly. I'm left in a sea of wedding finery, snacks, virgin mimosas, and my bride-to-be standing there in a wedding dress.

Grace wanted her to look like Cinderella and her wish came true. Calliope stands there in a dress with a tight bodice and a flowing skirt. Her hair is curled and pulled away from her face, pinned with beautiful, real pearl accessories. "Is everything okay?" Calliope asks, the hesitance in her voice a contrast from the confidence she had just moments before.

I cross the room and stand in front of her. "I love you, Calliope Jackson. That's it. You are everything that I have ever looked for and everything I hope to cherish for the rest of my life. No one else fills my soul like you. No one else makes me feel whole." I recite my vows to her in the privacy of her hotel room. "You are the love of my life and I want nothing more than to share my triumphs and challenges with you for the rest of my life. I promise that I will make the struggle I put you through worth it. Worth the energy, worth the time, and worth your love. Because we are far from normal, but I hope that that's the tie that bonds us."

Her tongue parts her lips, leaving them wet in its wake. The shine of tears makes her green eyes watery. "You're crazy, you know that," she whispers. "I've known it since the day we met."

I pull her closer until the fabric of her wedding dress crushes against my suit. "Crazy for you, Calliope."

She stands on her toes, taller now that she's in heels. She plants the smallest, most intimate kiss on the side of my mouth. "What more could a girl ask for?"

18

CALLIOPE

7 MONTHS LATER

"You fucking piece of shit." I am who I am. I will not apologize for that. I will say what I feel and if that upsets Raniero, so be it. But I'm in labor and it fucking -*hurts*.

Raniero holds my hand in the car as he races down highway 24. "We're going to be at the hospital in five minutes," he swears. His fingers wrap around mine like a vice. "Give me all your pain, baby. Make me feel it. Squeeze my hand until you break it."

Who am I to tell him no? The next contraction that rocks through my uterus gets linked to how tightly I wring my hand around his. He blows through a red light and as we pass under a particularly bright part of the road, I can see his jaw tighten. "That's right," he growls through his teeth, "you make me hurt like you hurt, baby."

"I think I'm being ripped apart from the inside out, Raniero." My gritted teeth match his, but that's because my uterus feels like it's being torn out.

He tries to smile, but he's keeping his eyes on the road. I didn't expect to go into labor at 3:00 am when the rain was pouring down, but Raniero is handling it like a pro. He keeps the car straight and it doesn't drift for a second when he turns fast and tight off the highway and onto a backstreet to the hospital. "When we get to the hospital, you'll get an epidural and it'll be fine. You'll be out of pain in no time at all."

No time at all turns into an hour. First, they have to find out how close my contractions are. Then they check to see my dilation and progression. When they finally call the anesthesiologist, he's in another part of the hospital. It feels like forever before he arrives to put me out of my misery.

Being drugged is sheer bliss.

Despite my contractions coming every three minutes like clockwork, I was only five centimeters dilated. They put me in my own labor and delivery room and sent a nurse to check on me every half hour.

"Can I get you anything?" Raniero is like an anxious puppy. He goes from sitting in the proffered chair by the hospital to standing by my side and squeezing my hand. His eyes watch my belly and he nervously rummages around in the 'go bag' when I ask him for my phone. "I-I don't remember grabbing it."

For the first time in the months we've been together, he looks genuinely distressed. Gone is the calm, cool, and collected Valenti that casually pulled a gun on me at my open house. In his place is a fretful and anxious man that looks left, right, and center when he can't find my phone.

"It's in my jacket," I remind him dreamily. The doctor said the epidural wouldn't put me to sleep, but it would certainly lessen the pain and I might fall asleep anyway. "I just wanna text my dad."

Raniero is halfway to bringing my phone back to me when I say those words. Then he stops in the middle of the room and holds the phone up next to his head. "Uh, what? Calli, baby, maybe we should wait until we're back home."

He's remembering the wedding. After we exchanged vows in the hotel room, a little private ceremony between the two of us, we headed to the church a few blocks away where a bevy of police cars were waiting for us. My father, who'd been invited, was nowhere to be found, but all of his buddies were. They said they'd received a tip that Raniero Valenti had held me captive against my will.

I don't know if my father knew or if he just suspected it, but either way, Raniero had to clear his name before the festivities were allowed to start. I lied with my hand on a Bible that he never kept me captive. I'd go to hell one day for those lies, but at least my life on earth would be pretty nice for a while.

"It's okay," I reach out to grab my phone from him even though he's nowhere close to me. "We'll be okay. I just want to tell him that I'm going to be a better parent than he ever was." If I had my mother's phone number, I'd text her, too.

I know why she left all those years ago, but I'll never forgive her for leaving me and my brothers behind. Apollo and Ares were old enough to defend themselves against dad, but I was still young. I was still abused by him until the day I left the house.

Raniero sighs heavily, making it clear that he doesn't approve of what I'm doing, but ultimately, he crosses the rest of the room and hands me the phone. "If he sends the police here, Calliope, I swear to God," he threatens.

If my father sends the police to the hospital, I don't know what I'll do. I've never been the type to fight back against him, but that will change now that I have a family to protect.

It takes me a few minutes to type up a suitable message. My fingers feel slow and my brain feels thick with fog. But in the end, I press send on my last communication with the man that almost ruined my life.

> Your grandson is about to be born. If it wasn't for you, I wouldn't be having my happy ending. Thanks for all that you've done. Thanks for all the times you beat sense into me, literally. You made me stronger. Strong enough to know that I will move heaven and earth to keep this baby safe from you. Strong enough to protect him and all my future kids from men like you. You'll never see your grandson, not as long as I have anything to say about it. I hope you're happy now that you've driven everyone away.

I toss my phone onto the side table and let Raniero be my strength for the rest of my labor. Five hours pass before I'm dilated enough to push. The nurse holds one of my legs and Raniero holds the other. With the doctor in front of me coaching me to push, my husband looks me in the eyes and mouths the same words.

Sweat drips down my forehead like a waterfall. I grab onto the railings of the bed for support. Every time I bear down to push, the pressure grows. The epidural withholds most of the pain, but I can still feel my son as he crowns. My body feels like it's being opened up. There is no stabbing, tearing pain, just tension and heaviness as our son is born.

"And... he's here!" The doctor says with an excited look on her face. She lifts his little body up enough for me to see him. He's covered in placenta and blood, but he looks beautiful. "What's his name, mama?"

Raniero and I talked about this at length before he was born. I wasn't partial to anything in particular, so he presented me with a list of names that he'd always wanted for his son.

"Gabriel," I breathe out with what remaining energy I have, "we decided on Gabriel." I lay back against the pillows that are now soaked in my sweat.

"You did such a great job," Raniero praises me. His eyes sparkle with tears, the first I've ever witnessed. "You were strong and brave and beautiful every step of the way."

I know I look like hell and I call him on it. "Shut up," I groan, "I look like shit."

But he brings his hand up to my forehead to remove the bits of hair that stuck to the sweat on my brow. Then Raniero leans forward and presses his lips to the sweaty patch of skin. "You look like a mother, Calliope, and that is certainly the most beautiful sight I've ever seen."

The doctor interrupts our sweet moment to ask if Raniero wants to cut the cord. He leaves me only for a second, but I watch him with fascinated eyes as he transforms before me.

Raniero stands in front of our son openly weeping. He whispers a few Italian prayers over Gabriel before cutting the cord and freeing him.

The man that less than a year ago forced me to walk around on a leash and crawl on my hands and knees like a dog has a soul after all.

"I love you, Raniero," I close my eyes and let the exhaustion wash over me like a wave.

I barely feel his hand enclose mine. I'm falling asleep when he's saying, "I love you, too, Calliope Valenti."

I don't snooze forever, just for a few minutes before my after-birth needs to be passed. But by the time I open my eyes, Gabriel has been cleaned up and wrapped in a blanket.

"Skin-to-skin time, mama," the doctor coos as she hands my son to me for the first time. She starts to remove the blanket, allowing his tiny, precious little body to be pressed against me. "He's beautiful. You did an amazing job."

Gabriel has all the best qualities of his father and me. He has Raniero's bone structure and my green eyes. His cheeks are full and pink and he stares at me as if I'm the eighth wonder of the world. He looks at me just like his father does.

"Thank you," Raniero whispers as he comes closer and gets as close to us as the bed will allow. "This is truly the happiest moment of my life."

And he's right. My body feels dead and I think I could sleep for three days if I wanted to. But holding my son with my husband staring at the both of us lovingly is better than sleep. It's better than everything. It's perfect.

19

RANIERO

3 MONTHS LATER

Gabriel is down for the night. And by down for the night I mean he's going to wake up in two and a half hours searching for mom's boob.

"How'd he do?" Calliope asks as I come out of his nursery. For the first month, she insisted on putting him to bed every night herself. I was allowed to be in the room, but she couldn't bear to be separated from him for even a minute. When we entered the second month, I could see her starting to drag. The bags under her eyes were growing darker by the day and it was harder to get her to speak to me when the two of us were alone.

Grace was the one that helped me realize she

was suffering from a mild form of postpartum depression. Though I changed diapers, got up with him in the night, and held him as often as she'd let me, Calliope still felt like a majority of the work fell on her shoulders. She was the feeding machine, after all, and it wiped her energy.

It was tough to convince her to spend a few hours away from Gabriel and go to a spa in town, but when I told her that my brothers would come over to help and we'd have Grace in the kitchen if we really needed help, she reluctantly agreed. Things improved after that. She'd even started letting me put him to bed myself.

"He did great," I reassure her. "No need to worry. He was a perfect angel." Unlike his nap earlier when he kicked and screamed until he fell asleep with tears on his cheeks. Gabriel hated sleeping. He wanted to be awake all the time so that he could see everything. He fought sleep like it was his arch nemesis, a feeling that I understood all too well.

"Good," Calliope breathes a sigh of relief. "I was afraid he was going to give you trouble."

I come to the couch where she's sitting in our bedroom and take the spot down by her feet. "If he gives me trouble, I'll give it right back," I threaten with a smile. Surreptitiously, I grab her foot and start to rub her arch. Calliope's eyes roll back into her head as she leans back and enjoys the massage. "How are you doing, by the way? Remember, we need to talk so I can meet all of your needs."

She nods her head and says that I don't need to remind her. "It was just a dark few weeks after Gabriel was born. The doctor said at my six-week check-up that that's normal. My hormones were starting to stabilize and I was fully healed. It's natural to feel a little out of sorts."

I don't remind her that at one point, she didn't talk to me for three days straight. She walked around the house like a zombie and I was afraid for her well-being and mental health. "Of course. But let me know if you need a day to yourself. I'll have the boys here in no time. Stefano has been begging for a day with Gabe to pick up chicks."

Calliope snorts and I swear I see her eyes roll as she raises her head to stare at me. "He's not using our son to pick up girls," she says with a shake of her head. "He can get plenty of women without Gabe's help."

I cluck my tongue at her. "But those green eyes, Calli," I pout, "they're a lady magnet." I should know; her green eyes attract me to her every day.

She doesn't say anything else, just lolls her head about as I switch feet.

"He's a good baby, Calliope. You're a wonderful mother to him and we're all so blessed to have Gabriel in our lives. My mother says she's making another trip next month just to spend some time with him." Gabriel is her first grandchild and though she spent three weeks here after he was born, she can't wait to come out and see him again. She's been talking about moving back to the states to be around him more, but dad has been keeping her grounded in Italy.

Calliope nods her head softly. "I'm happy to hear that, really. It's just," she pauses, "I just feel." Calliope doesn't know how to finish the sentence, so she just sighs in frustration.

I release her foot and let my hand trail up as high as it will go. I wrap my fingers around her calf and squeeze. "Tell me, Calli. Tell me what you're feeling or what you want. I'm here for you."

She gives me a wan little smile before tilting her head to the side. For a few moments, Calliope is quiet. I see the wheels in her head churning as she thinks about how to say what's on her mind. Then after a bit, she figures it out. "Does it make me a bad mom if I can't stop thinking about having sex with my husband?"

Ding dong, my cock is knocking on the front door of my pants. "Uh, um," I clear my throat, "no, of course not." I've been gentle with her since Gabriel's birth. She was cleared to have sex after her sixth week postpartum, but she was too tired. For another couple of weeks, we struggled through her exhaustion before finally having sex for the first time. It didn't last long and when we were done, she grabbed a bag of peas and held them to her crotch. Her stitches from tearing might have dissolved weeks ago, but the pressure of all the blood rushing to her vagina was nearly unbearable.

We tried again a few times and the result was always the same. It was like the spark of our pre-baby days had disappeared. Calliope was always icing her swollen vulva and swearing that it would get better in time. Or at least she hoped it would considering that's what the doctor told her. I didn't expect her desire to come back so quickly.

"We've just been so gentle and sweet with one another," she explains after a few seconds. "It's been very nice. I just miss feeling you buried to the hilt inside of me. I miss your weight on top of me. I miss all of it."

My dick is screaming at me to rip off my pants and impale her right now. "I just don't want to hurt you, Calliope." That didn't stop me before, but it does now that she's in such a fragile state. "You're always icing your vagina and that's just from a few minutes of gentle thrusting."

Calliope leans forward and though the exhaustion weighs heavily on the bags under her eyes, I see a glint of desire in her gaze. "Then give me a good reason to ice my pussy, Raniero."

God, I love it when she uses dirty words. "Calliope," I start.

"What?" She taunts. "Do you not find me attractive anymore now that I'm the mother of your child?"

That couldn't be further from the truth. I found her the sexiest in the hospital room the day she gave birth. Knowing that she had given me my heart's greatest desire had made me the hardest I'd ever been in my life. I rubbed one out in the bathroom after everything was said and done because I knew it would be a while before I was back inside of her.

"Calliope, you are the sexiest, most beautiful woman imaginable. If you've anything post-Gabriel, it's even hotter than before." I'd stay buried inside of her forever if I could, but I have responsibilities and duties.

She grabs the hem of her shirt and slowly lifts it up, revealing her naked breasts. "Then show me," she says as she discards the fabric on the floor. "Show me how sexy I am to you, Raniero."

It's a cry for lust; it's a cry for help. I can see it in the way her eyes twinkle. Calliope wants to know she's still beautiful to me because she doesn't necessarily feel beautiful to herself.

I'm happy to remind her that she's the love of my life. I'd do it every day, three times a day if I could. And when I'm fucking her tight, sweet little pussy, she screams, "Put another baby in me, Raniero." And I come on the spot filling her center with my hot, fertile seed.

We agreed to wait until Gabriel was six months old before we tried for another baby, but she knows what I like. She knows I want to breed her like a prized racehorse. And when Calliope speaks those words, I can't help but orgasm on the spot.

I mark her with my seed, a reminder that no other man will trespass here as long as I'm alive. Calliope is mine. I am like a greedy child that's obsessed with my possessions. And just over a year ago, I captured the best possession of all: Calliope.

It has been the greatest year of my life and I can't wait for the next 365 days. And the 365 days after that. The rest of my life is laid out in front of me. I get to have a family. I get to run my empire. I get to fuck the most beautiful woman in the world.

I am the luckiest man alive.

HAVE YOU LEFT A REVIEW?

Reviews are an author's bread and butter. This is how new readers find us and how old readers determine if a new series is worth their time. If you enjoyed this book, take a moment to leave a review or put in a recommendation on BookBub.

FOLLOW KELSIE CALLOWAY

Sign up for my newsletter and stay up-to-date on my new releases. Newsletters include links to new books, sales, freebies, bonus content, and more. I also include promo materials for free book giveaways and links to books by other authors. Newsletters are sent once a week and you are welcome to unsubscribe at any time. :)

Newsletter: https://geni.us/KelsieCallowayNL

www.ingramcontent.com/pod-product-compliance
Lightning Source LLC
Chambersburg PA
CBHW072227150726
48002CB00005B/1975